The Mar

The Marquise of O–

Heinrich von Kleist

Translated by Richard Stokes

ET REMOTISSIMA PROPE

100 PAGES

100 PAGES

Published by Hesperus Press Limited

4 Rickett Street, London SW6 1RU

www.hesperuspress.com

The Marquise of O– first published in German as *Die Marquise von O–* in 1808;
The Earthquake in Chile first published in German as *Jeronimo und Josephe: Eine
Scene aus dem Erdbeben zu Chili* in 1807; *The Foundling* first published in German
as *Der Findling* in 1811

This translation first published by Hesperus Press Limited, 2003

Introduction and English language translation © Richard Stokes, 2003

Foreword © Andrew Miller, 2003

ISBN: 1-84391-054-3

CONTENTS

I was nineteen when I first read Kleist's stories. I was working at a vegetable-canning factory in Holland. The workers, transients from every part of Europe, lived in a marquee with a palette floor. Spare palettes were used to make low-walled rooms, little evil-smelling nests of sleeping bags, backpacks, boots, cheese rind, cigarette butts, beer bottles. I still have the paperback edition of Kleist that I read there, the pages impressively weathered and starting to peel from the spine. I had picked up the book as part of a haphazard attempt to educate myself in European literature, a subject I knew almost nothing about when I left school. I don't know why I should have chosen Kleist rather than some of the bigger, more obvious names from the pantheon, but one reason must have been the parallels I saw between Kleist's life and Georg Büchner's, the only other Germanophone writer I knew anything about (I was in a school production of Büchner's *Leonce and Lena*). Though they were not strictly contemporaries of each other – Büchner was born two years after Kleist's death – both lived in that period of intellectual and social ferment between the French Revolution and the Europe-wide uprisings of 1848. Both were disappointed idealists. Both lived fitful, restless existences. Both died young: Büchner from typhus at the age of twenty-three; Kleist by his own hand at thirty-four. In each case their work – quite modest outputs – was fully valued only after their deaths. Posthumous victories, slightly sad, though to a nineteen-year-old apprentice writer their black fate was their glamour. I was, in those days, more inclined to admire unhappiness.

On first reading the stories my favourite was *Michael Kohlhaas*, a tale of obsession and warped justice set in the petty states of sixteenth-century Germany, not collected here but well worth seeking out. 'The Marquise of O–' seemed, by comparison, almost flippant, and re-reading it after twenty-three years I was still unsure what I should make of it. What I *could* make of it. A love story that has at its heart a rape. A melodrama that teeters on the edge of farce. Everyone is in the grip of uncontrollable emotions. They suffer convulsions, they weep profusely, they are astonished beyond measure and weak from swooning. Late in the story the Marquise's brother wonders whether his sister's impetuous Russian suitor has gone 'quite out of his mind'. But the point, surely, is that they are all in the same condition, a household of hysterics who run in and out of doors, strike poses, rage at each other, mouth extravagant curses. There is comedy here, though how much is intended it's hard to say. The ending is of the 'happily ever after' sort. All parties are reconciled; life will go on smoothly now. We're hurried out with talk of babies, handsome bequests. None of it quite convinces. And what was the point of it all? Was it just an anecdote? A newspaper clipping of the human interest kind, padded out by a clever young writer? What did he think he had done?

To make more sense of the piece, for the story to resonate as I believe it can, it needs to be read in the context of Kleist's more 'typical' productions, and the two stories presented here alongside 'The Marquise of O–' do this admirably. Shorter and darker, these stories, particularly 'The Earthquake in Chile' – a wonderful and disturbing work, marvellously concentrated – are visions of physical and moral chaos. The lovers caught in the earthquake and its aftermath are not saved by their youth or their innocence. Indeed, their virtue seems to make them more of a target; their fate is shocking in its violence and injustice. Malign human forces are at work here, but Nature, destroying the city of Santiago as it destroyed, twenty-two years before Kleist's birth, the city of Lisbon, is no gentler. The story is angry, blasphemous. In its directness, its refusal to offer more than a grain or two of consolation, it has a tough, modern feel to it. View the 'Marquise' through the blood and rubble of the 'Earthquake', and the story acquires an edginess, an air of the absurd, that makes it very much more interesting – to this reader at least. The confusion into which the family is thrown by the Marquise's inexplicable pregnancy is model and symptom of a larger confusion. The commandant, his unpleasant wife, the tightly buttoned brother, the overwrought Count, are hemmed in by a darkness no rational enquiry, no effort of the intelligence can ever dispel. This is what explains the unease that runs like a current of chill water through the story's conclusion. How can things be put right? In such a world all reconciliations are temporary and contingent.

The Foundling completes the triptych. Here is villainy, sexual scheming, violence – all good Kleistian obsessions. Piachi's humanity in rescuing Nicolo from the plague, in taking the boy into his house and bringing him up as a son, comes to nothing. The story ends, as the story of Michael Kohlhaas ends, on a scaffold, but whereas the quasi-mad Kohlhaas goes calmly to the block, Piachi rages to the last, refusing absolution in order that he might sink into hell to continue his vengeance, like Ugolino gnawing at the skull of Archbishop Ruggeri in Dante's *Inferno*.

These are not comfortable stories; Kleist was not a comfortable man. A failed soldier, a failed civil servant, a failed editor (despite early success), a failed son. In the end he was estranged even from his beloved sister Ulrike. He craved order and clarity but soon ceased to believe such things were possible. His last days in the company of the terminally ill

Mme Vogel, were, according to the testimony of witnesses at Wannsee, happy ones. I hope so. His literary ghost is there in Kierkegaard, in Kafka, Thomas Mann, Camus, the Theatre of the Absurd. He certainly became a part of my own literary make-up, part of that colouring we call influence. This new translation of his work is very welcome – the more so for coming in an edition small enough for anyone's backpack.

– Andrew Miller, 2003

INTRODUCTION

Heinrich von Kleist was born on 18th October 1777. One of seven children, he came from an ancient military family, and his father was a company commander in the garrison town of Frankfurt an der Oder. Kleist became an officer cadet in the French campaign of 1793, and in March 1797 was granted a commission in the Guards Regiment. Two years later, despite his engagement to Wilhelmine von Zenge, he violated the family tradition, resigned his commission and began to devote himself entirely to what he called his 'moral education'. He cultivated an interest in music and philosophy and studied science and mathematics at Frankfurt University, where he became acquainted with the works of Fichte and other philosophers. Although this was the Age of Enlightenment, he confided in a celebrated letter to his half-sister Ulrike that he had little faith in man's ability to shape his own destiny – thus adumbrating one of the main themes of his writing.

This pessimism increased when he began to read the philosophical writings of Immanuel Kant, while working as a civil-service volunteer in the Department of Economics in Berlin. Kant's rejection of the idea that the world develops according to a plan, predestined by God, which will lead to perfection, had a shattering impact on Kleist's confidence. In a letter to his fiancée, dated 23rd March 1801, he summarised his reaction to the Kantian perception that human understanding is limited to the empirical facts of man's finite existence, in these despairing words:

'We cannot decide whether what we call truth is truly true ('*das, was wir Wahrheit nennen, wahrhaft Wahrheit ist*') or whether it only appears so to us. If the latter is the case, then the truth that we gather here on earth no longer exists in death – and all our efforts to acquire a possession which will follow us into the grave are vain. Alas, Wilhelmine, if this sharp thought does not pierce your heart, do not laugh at another, whom it has wounded to the depths of his sacred being. My only, my highest aim has vanished and now I possess none –'

With his trust in the force of reason shattered, Kleist was now confronted with the incomprehensibility of existence. Kant's *Kritik der reinen Vernunft* [*Critique of Pure Reason*] had a devastating effect on the poet, who had until now maintained that man could guide the powers that ruled his life; but after his idiosyncratic reading of Kant's *Critique* (he seems to ignore those passages in which Kant suggests that there are other ways of becoming aware of the essence of things), he recognised the fallacy of such a claim, considered that metaphysical reflections on the nature of human existence were pointless, and concluded that man, instead of basing his life on abstract principles, should concentrate instead on performing his duty. Kant's categorical imperative (*'Erfülle deine Pflicht'*, 'Do your duty'), however, was of little value to a man who had no idea of what that duty was. Plunged into despair, he now led a roving existence, and seemed incapable of settling; he considered devoting his life to study; entertained the idea of entering the Prussian civil service; thought of buying a farm in Switzerland; broke off his engagement to Wilhelmine; decided to travel. And became a writer.

The Kant 'crisis' had released his poetic powers, and in the next decade that led to his suicide he wrote the works – ten plays, eight *Novellen*, several articles and a number of aphorisms and essays, none of which received any proper recognition during his lifetime – for which he is now famous. Many of these works bear witness to his profound pessimism and his attempts to come to terms with personal depression. The earliest of the plays, *Die Familie Schroffenstein* [*The Schroffenstein Family*] (1803), was written in the wake of his Kant crisis, and deals with human misunderstandings and the destructive power of chance: two Romeo-and-Juliet-like families wipe out one another in the course of a quarrel over the family estate. Kleist's first comedy, *Der zerbrochene Krug* [*The Broken Pitcher*], was written between 1803 and 1807, and deals with the fallibility of human feeling and the corrupt nature of human justice. *Amphitryon* (1807) is much more than an adaptation of Molière's play (1668) of the same name, and its main theme is, typically, the confused feelings of a woman (Alkmene) who, although she loves her husband (Amphitryon), is also loved by Jupiter, who visits her one night in the guise of her husband. Forced to decide between the two, she chooses Jupiter – because of the highly charged emotional experience of the lovemaking – and reviles the true Amphitryon. When told of the true state of affairs, she pronounces a curse on her senses and feelings, and is overwhelmed by despair and confusion. *Penthesilea*, a one-act tragedy of some three thousand lines of blank verse, also dates from 1807 and reverses the legend of Achilles slaying the Amazon Penthesilea during the Trojan War. The fallibility of human feelings is once again revealed as the Amazon Queen, mistaking Achilles' love for scorn, sets her hounds on him and joins them in tearing his body apart.

Kleist was by now becoming known, and there was nothing that he courted more than the approval of Goethe, who had already mounted a (disastrous) production of *The Broken Pitcher* in Weimar. Early in 1808 Kleist sent Goethe, 'on the knees of his heart', the 'organic fragment' of *Penthesilea*, but Goethe's response was no more than lukewarm. Kleist's Dionysian temperament was at odds with Goethe's classicism, and the gulf between them was deepened when, during the second half of 1808, Kleist wrote *Die Hermannsschlacht*, the plot of which is nothing less than an appeal to Germans and Austrians to rise up against foreign oppression and punish all pro-Napoleonic traitors. Goethe was a fervent admirer of Napoleon, and the publication of *Die Hermannsschlacht* led to an irrevocable rupture.

War broke out in April 1809 and Kleist observed at first hand Napoleon's first setback at the Battle of Aspern. A year later he finished what is arguably his finest drama, *Prinz Friedrich von Homburg*, a play which deals with the clash between the individual and society, and the realisation that moral and spiritual values can only be established when the individual has freed himself from subjective desires. Although *Prinz Friedrich von Homburg* was his final play, it was not his final work. At various times between 1808 and 1810 Kleist had written a number of stories, which he now revised and prepared for publication. They were collected in two volumes in the autumn of 1810 and in June 1811, and included *Die Marquise von O–* ['The Marquise of O–'], *Das Erdbeben in Chili* ['The Earthquake in Chile'], and *Der Findling* ['The Foundling'].

The earliest of these *Novellen* was probably 'The Earthquake in Chile', which was first published in five instalments in Cotta's *Morgenblatt für gebildete Stände* during September 1807 as *Jeronimo und Josephe: Eine Scene aus dem Erdbeben zu Chili*. Kleist's source for the story remains unknown, but many details of the *Novelle* must have been suggested by descriptions of the Lisbon earthquake of 1755. It is, of course, not the earthquake itself that attracted Kleist's attention, but the themes that it allowed him to explore. What better way to address the incomprehensible forces that rule the universe than to depict how an earthquake is required to save the lives of two innocent lovers who had been condemned to death, and who are then butchered on the final page? Scenes of great peace and beauty are juxtaposed with scenes of indescribable horror – natural horror in the case of the earthquake, and human horror in the cathedral where the lovers are lynched by a frenzied mob. On the penultimate page Don Fernando, with his battered son lying dead at his feet, raises his eyes to heaven. What is the reader to make of such a gesture? Is it grief? Or revolt against a cruel God? Or simply the uncomprehending reaction of someone faced with such horror?

Similar extremes are encountered in 'The Marquise of O–', a story that first appeared in the second number of *Phöbus* in February 1808. The first number of the same journal had published *Penthesilea*, which had greatly shocked its readers. This time they were outraged by the seemingly lubricious story of a young widow who conceives a child without her knowledge, places an advertisement in the local newspaper, inviting the father to come forward, and waits for him to show up at her parents' house 'at eleven o'clock on the morning of the third'. Critics have spent much time searching for the sources of Kleist's *Novelle*, and several works have been cited: Montaigne's essay on drunkenness, in which a woman is raped in her sleep; Cervantes' *La fuerza de la sangre* [*The Power of Blood*], where a Spanish nobleman rapes a young woman while she is unconscious; and an anonymous story, *Die gerettete Unschuld* [*Rescued Innocence*], that appeared in the *Berlinisches Archiv der Zeit und ihres Geschmacks* in April 1798, which describes the rape of an apparently dead girl by a Bavarian merchant, and which, according to Alfred Klaar in *Heinrich von Kleist, Die*

Marquise von O: Die Dichtung und ihre Quellen, contains a number of phrases that appear almost verbatim in Kleist's story. The sources, however, are purely an academic matter, for Kleist is not interested in the rape – which he indicates by a mere dash – but rather the consequences of the rape, the reaction of human beings and human institutions to the crime, and the themes that the story allows him to explore: sex and violence; appearance and reality; the isolation of the individual; and the sanctity of human feelings in the face of upheaval and deceit.

Human institutions come off badly in many of Kleist's plays and *Novellen*: the Church in 'The Earthquake in Chile', for example, is depicted as bigoted and cruel; 'The Marquise of O–' shows the marchioness's family, before the final reconciliation, to be disunited and unsupportive; while the lawyers in 'The Foundling' are motivated by dubious personal concerns, and find in favour of the evil Nicolo. 'The Foundling' is, perhaps, the most depressing of all Kleist's stories, and though it was not published until 1811, in the second volume of his *Collected Stories*, it might well have been started in the wake of the Kant crisis which plunged Kleist into such despair. Whereas 'The Earthquake in Chile' ends with a ray of hope, as the infant Felipe survives, there is no such solace in 'The Foundling', which chronicles the disintegration of a philanthropic tradesman, Piachi, who rescues and adopts a plague-infested boy who, by the end of the story, has directly or indirectly caused the death of Piachi, his wife and his son, and has also dispossessed him of his house and possessions. Piachi murders his tormentor in an outburst of rage, and is hanged for his crime in the Piazza del Popolo; he goes willingly to his death, since his one desire is to go to hell to wreak revenge on the satanic foundling.

Kleist's depressing world is peopled by individuals who are wrenched out of their routine existence and thrown into a situation which is beyond their comprehension and control. The chaotic upheaval in his stories mirrors, perhaps, the havoc created in Europe by the outbreak of the French Revolution and the Napoleonic Wars. The chaos is also reflected in his extraordinary style. As we read his tortuous sentences, punctuated by endless subordinate clauses and adverbial phrases, we stumble along like his own bewildered characters; and just as they try to make sense of their lives, we attempt to unravel the complexities of his syntax. Some of Kafka's sentences are not dissimilar, and, like Kafka, Kleist is a poet of nightmare: chance unleashes irrational forces and drives individuals to the brink of despair, although, unlike in Kafka, chance can also work in the other direction and, as in 'The Marquise of O–', restore both equilibrium and happiness.

Kleist himself was not so fortunate. Although he was supported through his life by his half-sister Ulrike and his cousin Marie von Kleist, who tried to help him by using her influence at court, he succumbed to the depression that had never ceased to torment him since his first encounter with Kant. Despite the technical and artistic perfection of many of his works, his loss of faith in reason eventually drove him to despair and suicide. On the morning of 21st November 1811 he set out for the shores of the Wannsee in the company of Henriette Vogel, a married woman who was suffering from terminal cancer of the uterus. At her request he shot her so that she would suffer no more. He then killed himself. Before his suicide, he wrote a letter to Ulrike, dated '*Am Morgen meines Todes*' ['On the morning of my death'], which talks of reconciliation and states '*daß mir auf Erden nicht zu helfen war*' – 'that there was no help for me on earth'.

– Richard Stokes, 2003

The Marquise of O–

(Based on a true incident, the setting of which has been relocated from the north to the south)

In M**, an important town in northern Italy, the widowed Marquise of O**, a lady of excellent reputation and mother of several well-bred children, had the following announcement published in the newspapers: that she had, without knowing the cause, come to find herself in an interesting condition, that she wished the father of the child she was expecting to present himself; and that she was resolved, out of consideration for her family, to marry him. The lady who, compelled by irrevocable circumstances, had with such confidence taken so strange a step, thus exposing herself to the derision of all the world, was the daughter of Colonel G**, the commandant of the citadel at M**. Some three years earlier her husband, the Marquis of O**, to whom she was most fervently and tenderly devoted, had lost his life during a journey to Paris on family business. At the request of her esteemed mother, Frau von G**, she had, after his death, left the country estate at V**, where she had hitherto lived, and returned with her two children to the house of her father, the commandant. Here, for the next few years, she had led a most secluded life, devoting herself to art and reading, the education of her children and the care of her parents – until the ** War suddenly filled the neighbourhood with the armed forces of almost every power, Russians included. Colonel G**, who had orders to defend the citadel, asked his wife and daughter to withdraw either to his own country estate or to that of his son, in the vicinity of V**. But before the ladies had even concluded their deliberations, while they were still weighing up the suffering they would undergo in the fortress against the horrors they would be exposed to in the open country, the Russian troops overran the citadel, which was now called upon to surrender. The colonel announced to his family that he would act as if they were simply not present; and answered the Russians with bullets and grenades. The enemy replied by shelling the citadel. They set fire to the magazine, occupied an outwork, and when after repeated calls to surrender the commandant still hesitated, the enemy mounted a night attack and took the fortress by storm.

Just as the Russians, covered by heavy howitzer fire, were forcing a way in, the left wing of the commandant's residence burst into flames, and the women were compelled to leave. The colonel's wife, hurrying after her daughter, who was fleeing downstairs with her children, called out to her that they should all stay together and shelter in the underground vaults; but at that very moment a grenade exploded inside the house, throwing everything into the utmost confusion. The Marquise, with her two children, found herself in the outer precincts of the castle where the fighting was at its fiercest and where shots flashed through the night and, having no idea where to turn, she was forced back again into the burning building. Here, just as she was about to escape through the back door, she had the misfortune to encounter a troop of enemy snipers who, as soon as they noticed her, suddenly fell silent, slung their rifles over their shoulders and, with obscene gestures, carried her off. While the hideous rabble, fighting amongst themselves, tugged her to and fro, the Marquise screamed for help to her terrified womenfolk escaping through the gate – but in vain. They dragged her into the innermost courtyard where, suffering the most shameful assaults, she was about to sink to the ground, when a Russian officer, hearing her strident screams, appeared on the scene and, with furious blows of his sword, drove back the dogs from the prey for which they lusted. To the Marquise he seemed an angel sent from heaven. He drove the hilt of his sword into the face of one murderous brute, who still had his arms around her slender body, sending him reeling backwards with blood pouring from his mouth; he then addressed the lady courteously in French, offered her his arm and led her, speechless from all this commotion, into the other wing of the palace which the flames had not yet reached, where she now collapsed, completely unconscious. At this moment – since the Marquise's terrified servants presently arrived, he took steps to send for a doctor; assured them, as he replaced his hat, that she would soon recover; and returned to the fighting.

It was not long before the fortress was completely overrun; and the commandant – who had only continued to resist because he had been offered no amnesty – was already retreating with dwindling strength to the main gate, when the Russian officer, very flushed in the face, came through it and called on him to surrender. The commandant replied that he had only been waiting for such an order, surrendered his sword and requested permission to go into the castle and look for his family. The Russian officer, who, to judge from the part he was playing, seemed to be one of the leaders of the attack, gave him permission to do so, accompanied by a guard; took rather hasty command of the detachment, put an end to the fighting wherever the outcome still seemed to be in doubt, and gained immediate control of all the strong points of the citadel. Shortly afterwards he returned to the scene of battle, gave orders for the fire, which was beginning to spread furiously, to be extinguished, and joined in the work with miraculous energy whenever his orders were not carried out with proper zeal. At one moment he was clambering, hose in hand, along burning gables, directing the jet of water; at another he filled the hearts of his Asiatic compatriots with horror, as he stood in the arsenals, rolling out powder kegs and live grenades. The commandant, who had meanwhile entered the house, now learned of the misadventure that had befallen his daughter and became quite distraught. The Marquise, who had recovered from her fainting fit without the help of a doctor, as the Russian had predicted, and was so happy to see all her family alive and well that she only stayed in bed in deference to their excessive solicitude, assured her father that she had no other wish but to get up and express her gratitude to her saviour. She already knew that he was Count F**, lieutenant-colonel of the ** Rifle Corps and holder of the Distinguished Service Cross and several other orders. She asked her father to beg him most urgently not to leave the citadel without making a brief appearance in the castle. The commandant, who honoured his daughter's feelings, now returned at once to the fortifications where on the ramparts (he could find no better opportunity) he discovered the Count hurrying to and fro, occupied with a multitude of military tasks and reviewing his battered troops, and informed him of his grateful daughter's wish. The Count assured him that he was only waiting for a moment's respite from all his duties, to come and pay her his respects. He was just enquiring about the lady's health, when the reports of several officers tore him back again into the thick of the battle. At daybreak the commander-in-chief of the Russian troops appeared and inspected the citadel. He conveyed his respects to the commandant and expressed his regret that good fortune had not reinforced the latter's courage, and gave him permission, on his word of honour, to go wherever he wished. The commandant thanked him, and declared how much, in the course of this one day, he had been grateful to the Russians in general, and in particular to the young Count F**, lieutenant colonel of the t**n Rifle Corps. The general asked what had happened; and when he was informed of the outrageous assault on the commandant's daughter, he reacted with the utmost indignation. He summoned Count F** by name to come forward and, after a brief eulogy in which he praised him for his noble conduct, during which the Count blushed crimson, he concluded that he would have the shameful miscreants, who had disgraced the name of the Tsar, shot; and ordered the Count to reveal who they were. Count F** replied, in a confused speech, that he was not in a position to give their names, since the faint shimmer of the lamps in the castle courtyard had made it impossible for him to recognise their faces. The general, who had heard that the castle at the time in question had been ablaze, expressed amazement at this; remarked that people one knew well could, after all, be recognised in the dark by their voices; and ordered him, as the Count could only shrug his shoulders in embarrassment, to research the matter with the utmost zeal and rigour. At this moment someone pushed his way forwards through the assembled troops and reported that the commandant's servants had been able to drag one of the villains, who had been wounded by Count F** and had collapsed in a corridor, into a cell, where he was still being held. The general immediately had him brought under guard into his presence, where he was swiftly interrogated; and after the prisoner had identified his accomplices, the entire rabble, five in number, were shot. Having dealt with this matter, the general ordered his troops to withdraw from the citadel, leaving only a small garrison behind; the officers hurriedly went their separate ways and rejoined their own units; amid the confusion of this hasty withdrawal, the Count approached the commandant and expressed his regret that, in these circumstances, he could merely present his most respectful compliments to the Marquise; and in less than an hour the whole fortress was once more empty of Russian troops.

The family were now debating how they might in the future find an opportunity of somehow expressing their gratitude to the Count; they were horror-stricken, however, to learn that on the very day of his departure from the fortress, he had lost his life in a skirmish with enemy troops. The messenger who brought this news to M** had with his own eyes seen the Count, with a mortal bullet-wound in the chest, being carried to P**, where, according to reliable information, he had passed away just as his bearers were about to set him down. The commandant went in person to the post-house to find out in greater detail what had happened, and discovered that on the battlefield, at the very moment of being hit, the Count had cried out: 'Julietta! This bullet avenges you!' whereupon he closed his lips forever. The Marquise was inconsolable that she had let slip the opportunity of throwing herself at his feet. She reproached herself bitterly that when he had declined, probably out of modesty, to see her in the castle, she had not gone to visit him herself; pitied the unfortunate lady, her namesake, whom he had remembered at the very moment of his death, and tried in vain to discover her whereabouts, in order to inform her of this unhappy and moving event; and several months went by before she herself could forget him.

The whole family now had to leave their quarters, so that the Russian commander could take up residence there. They first considered going to the commandant's estate, for which the Marquise had a great affection; but as the colonel was not fond of country life, the family moved into a house in the town and furnished it as a permanent home. Everything now returned to normal. The Marquise resumed the education of her children that had been interrupted for so long and, as recreation, brought out once more her easel and her books – when she, normally the epitome of good health, fell victim to repeated indispositions, which made her unfit for company for weeks at a time. She suffered from nausea, giddiness and fainting fits, and had no idea what to make of her strange condition. One morning, when the family were taking tea, and her father had left the room for a moment, the Marquise, emerging from a long period of reverie, said to her mother: 'If a woman were to tell me that she felt as I have just felt, when I picked up this teacup, I would think to myself that she must be with child.' Frau von G** said that she did not understand her. The Marquise explained once more that she had just experienced a sensation identical to the one she had felt when pregnant with her second daughter. Frau von G** said that she might give birth to Fantasy, and laughed. 'Morpheus, at any rate,' replied the Marquise, 'or one of his attendant dreams, would be his father;' and likewise laughed. But the colonel returned, the conversation was interrupted, and the whole subject, since the Marquise recovered within a few days, was forgotten.

Soon after this, at a time when the commandant's son, Forstmeister von G**, a forestry official, was at home, a footman entered and, to the family's amazement, announced Count F**. 'Count F**!' exclaimed father and daughter simultaneously; and the astonishment rendered everyone speechless. The footman assured them that his eyes and ears had not deceived him, and that the Count was already waiting in the ante-room. The commandant himself leapt to his feet to let him in, whereupon the Count entered, his face a little pale, but looking as handsome as a young god. After the initial scene of uncomprehending astonishment was over, and the

Count had assured the parents, who had accused him of being dead, that he was alive, he turned to their daughter with great emotion in his face, and asked her before anything else how she felt. 'Very well,' replied the Marquise, who then wanted to know how he had come to life again. But *he*, who was not to be deflected, replied that she could not be telling him the truth, that her face looked strangely exhausted and that she, if he were not quite mistaken, was sick, and suffering. The Marquise, gladdened by the sincerity with which he voiced these concerns, replied that this exhaustion could, as a matter of fact, if he insisted, be taken for the after-effects of an infirmity she had suffered a few weeks ago; though she had no reason to fear that it would be of any further consequence. Whereupon he, with a passionate outbreak of joy, replied: 'neither had he!' and proceeded to ask her whether she would be willing to marry him. The Marquise did not know what to think of this conduct. Blushing deeply, she looked at her mother, and her mother looked with embarrassment at her son and her husband; while the Count went up to the Marquise and, taking her hand as though he wished to kiss it, asked again whether she had understood him. The commandant asked him if he would care to sit down, and, politely but rather gravely, placed a chair at his disposal. The colonel's wife said: 'We shall certainly continue to think you are a ghost until you reveal to us how you rose from the grave in which you were laid at P**.' The Count let go of the young lady's hand, sat down, and said that circumstances compelled him to be very brief; that he, mortally wounded in the chest, had been carried to P**; that for several months he had despaired of his life; that during this time he had never ceased to think of the Marquise; that he was unable to describe the mingling of joy and pain this vision had caused him; that he had finally, after his recovery, rejoined the army; that while there he had felt acutely ill at ease; that he had several times taken up his pen to relieve the turmoil of his heart by writing to the colonel and the Marquise; that he had suddenly been sent with dispatches to Naples; that he did not know whether he might not from there be summoned to Constantinople; that he might even have to go to St Petersburg; that he could not in the meantime continue to live without settling once and for all a certain matter that was upsetting his soul; that he had been unable to resist the impulse, as he was passing through M**, of taking a few steps towards fulfilling this aim; that, in short, he harboured the wish to be favoured with her hand, and begged them most respectfully, fervently and urgently to be kind enough to give him their answer on this point. The commandant, after a long pause, replied: that he felt very flattered by this proposal, if it was meant seriously, as he had no doubt that it was. His daughter had, however, on the death of her husband, the Marquis of O**, resolved not to embark on any second marriage. But since she had recently become so beholden to him, it was not out of the question that she might revise her decision in accordance with his wishes; for the time being, therefore, he would beg him on the Marquise's behalf to leave her a little time in which to ponder the matter in peace and quiet. The Count assured him that these kind sentiments did indeed fulfil all his hopes; that they would in different circumstances even satisfy him entirely; that he was fully aware of the great impropriety of finding them inadequate; that pressing circumstances, however, on which he was not in a position to elaborate, made it extremely desirable that he should have a more definite reply; that the horses which were to take him to Naples were already harnessed to his carriage; and that he would most fervently implore the colonel that if there was anything in this house which might speak in his favour – at which point he glanced at the Marquise – he should not be allowed to depart without some reassurance. The colonel, somewhat bewildered by such behaviour, replied that the gratitude the Marquise felt for him certainly entitled him to entertain great hopes, but not so great as these: she would not proceed without proper circumspection in taking a step on which the happiness of her whole life depended. It was imperative that his daughter, before committing herself, should have the pleasure of becoming better acquainted with him. He invited him, when he had finished travelling on business, to return to M** and spend some time as a guest in his family's house. If the Frau Marquise then felt that she could hope to find happiness through him, he, her father would then – and only then – be delighted to hear that she had given him a definite answer. The Count, growing red in the face, said that, during his entire journey here, he had predicted that this was bound to be the outcome of his impatient desires; that the distress into which it plunged him was nonetheless extreme; that, given the unfavourable role he was now being forced to play, he could only profit from closer acquaintance; that he felt he could answer for his reputation, if it was deemed necessary to take account of this most dubious of all attributes; that he was already taking steps to make amends for the one ignoble action, unknown to the world, that he had committed in his life; that he, in a word, was a man of honour, and begged them to accept his assurance that this assurance was the truth. The commandant replied, with a faint smile but without irony, that he endorsed all these statements. Never had he made the acquaintance of any young man who had in so short a time revealed so many admirable qualities of character. He was almost sure that a brief period of reflection would banish the indecision that still prevailed; but until there had been consultation with his own and the Count's family, he could give no other answer than the one he had already given. Whereupon the Count replied that his parents were no longer alive and that he was his own master. His uncle, General K**, would be sure to consent to the marriage. He added that he possessed a substantial fortune and would be prepared to make Italy his home. The commandant bowed courteously, reiterated his wishes, and requested that the matter should not be further discussed until after the Count's journey. The Count, after a short pause in which he displayed every sign of intense agitation, remarked, turning to the Marquise's mother, that he had done his utmost to avoid being sent on this journey; that he had taken the most decisive steps to this end, venturing to approach both the commander-in-chief and his uncle General K**; but that it had been their belief that this journey would shake him out of the melancholy which still remained from his illness; and that it was now plunging him into a state of utter wretchedness. The family did not know how to react to this statement. The Count, wiping his brow, added that if there were any hope it would bring him nearer to his heart's desire, he would try to postpone his journey for a day or perhaps even longer. And as he spoke he looked in turn at the commandant, the Marquise and her mother. Displeased, the commandant looked to the ground, lowered his gaze and did not answer him. His wife said: 'Go, go, dear Count, journey to Naples; and if on the way back you honour us for a time with your company, everything else will look after itself.' The Count sat for a moment, and appeared to wonder what he ought to do. Then, getting to his feet and setting aside his chair, he said that since he now recognised that the hopes with which he had entered the house were over-hasty, and since the family insisted on closer acquaintance – something of which he did not disapprove – he would return his dispatches to the headquarters at Z**, for them to be delivered by somebody else, and accept their kind offer to spend a few weeks as a guest in this, their family home. Whereupon he remained standing by the wall, with the chair in his hand, and looked at the commandant. The commandant replied that he would be extremely sorry if the Count, as a result of the passion which he had apparently conceived for his daughter, were to expose himself to the gravest of consequences; that he, however, presumably knew best what he should do and not do, and should therefore send off his dispatches and move into the rooms which were at his disposal. On hearing this, the Count was seen to change colour, kiss respectfully Frau von G**'s hand, bow to the others and withdraw.

When he had left the room, the family were at a loss to know what to make of such a display. Frau von G** said that the Count, having set out for Naples with dispatches, could not possibly wish to send them back to Z**, simply because on his way through M** he had not succeeded, in a five-minute conversation, to extract a promise of marriage from a lady with whom he was totally unacquainted. The Forstmeister expressed the view that for such a frivolous action he would at the very least be arrested and confined to barracks! And cashiered as well, the commandant added. But in fact, he continued, there was no such danger. This had merely been a warning salvo, and he would certainly come to his senses before actually sending back the dispatches. Frau von G**, when she heard of this danger, expressed the liveliest fear that he would in fact do so. It seemed to her that his headstrong, single-minded nature would be capable of precisely such an act. She most earnestly entreated her son to go after the Count

14

at once and prevent him from carrying out such a potentially calamitous act. The Forstmeister replied that such a move would have the opposite effect, and merely strengthen his hopes of gaining victory through stealth. The Marquise was of the same opinion, though she was convinced that, if her brother did not take this action, the dispatches would most definitely be returned, since the Count would sooner risk the consequences than compromise his honour. All agreed that his behaviour was very strange, and that he seemed to be in the habit of storming ladies' hearts like fortresses. At this moment the commandant noticed that the Count's harnessed carriage was standing ready outside the front door. He called his family to the window and asked one of the servants, who was just entering the room, whether the Count was still in the house. The servant answered that he was downstairs in the servants' quarters, in the company of an adjutant, writing letters and sealing packages. The commandant, suppressing his consternation, hurried downstairs with the Forstmeister and, seeing the Count working on tables that were not appropriate for his business, asked him whether he would not like to enter his own rooms. And whether there was anything else he required. The Count, continuing to write with great zeal, replied that he was most humbly obliged but had now completed his business; asked what the time was, as he sealed his letter; and wished the adjutant a safe journey, after he had handed him the entire portfolio. The commandant, who could not believe his eyes, said as the adjutant was leaving the house: 'Count, unless you have weighty reasons –' 'Compelling ones!' cried the Count, interrupting him; he accompanied the adjutant to the carriage and opened the door for him. 'In that case,' continued the commandant, 'I would at least send the dispatches –' 'Impossible,' answered the Count, while he helped the adjutant into his seat. 'The dispatches count for nothing in Naples without me. I have thought of that too. Drive on!' 'And your uncle's letters, sir?' called the adjutant, leaning out of the carriage door. 'Will reach me in M**,' replied the Count. 'Drive on!' said the adjutant, and the carriage sped away.

Count F** then turned to the commandant and asked him if he would kindly have him shown to his room. The bewildered colonel replied that it would be an honour to do so at once, summoned his own and the Count's servants, told them to see to the latter's luggage and conducted him to the apartments reserved for guests, where he took his leave without a smile. The Count changed his clothes, left the house to announce his presence to the military governor, and was not seen in the house for the whole of the rest of that day, until he returned shortly before dinner.

The family, meanwhile, were most distraught. The Forstmeister described how unequivocal the Count's replies had been when the commandant had conversed with him; his actions seemed to be totally premeditated; what on earth could be the motive, he asked, for such a whirlwind wooing? The commandant said that he could make neither head nor tail of it, and asked the family not to mention the matter again in his presence. Frau von G** kept on looking out of the window to see whether the Count was coming back to express regret for his recklessness, and repair the damage he had done. Eventually, when it grew dark, she sat down at the Marquise's side, who was working most industriously at a table and seemed to be avoiding all conversation. While the commandant was pacing up and down, she asked her in a low voice whether she had any idea of how this matter would end. 'If only her father could have prevailed on him to go to Naples, all would have been well!' the Marquise replied, with a timid glance towards the commandant. 'To Naples!' exclaimed her father, who had heard this remark. 'Should I have sent for a priest? Or had him arrested, locked up, and sent to Naples under guard?' 'No,' answered his daughter, 'but spirited protestations can be effective;' and she looked down rather angrily at her work again. The Count finally reappeared towards nightfall. The family fully expected that, after a preliminary exchange of courtesies, the matter would be discussed once more, and that they would implore him unanimously to revoke, if it were still possible, the intrepid step he had taken. But throughout the entire dinner they waited in vain for an opportunity. Deliberately avoiding anything that could lead to such a topic, the Count conversed with the commandant about the war, and with the Forst-meister about hunting. When he mentioned the battle at P**, during which he had been wounded, Frau von G** persuaded him to talk about his illness, asking him how he had prospered in so small a place, and whether he had been provided with all the appropriate comforts. He answered by telling them of various interesting details concerning his passion for the Marquise: how, during his illness, she had been constantly present at his bedside; how in the feverish delirium caused by his wound, he had had visions of her, and had kept confusing her with the image of a swan which, as a boy, he had seen on his father's estate; that he remembered with particular emotion one occasion on which he had pelted this swan with mud, whereupon she had silently dived beneath the surface, and had re-emerged washed clean by the water; that she had always seemed to be floating on watery fire, and that he had called out to her 'Tinka!', which had been the name of the swan, but that he had been unable to entice her towards him, since she had been content merely to glide about, arching her neck and thrusting out her breast; and then, blushing crimson, he suddenly declared that he loved her beyond all measure; whereupon he looked down again at his plate, and fell silent. The time finally came to rise from the table; and since the Count, after a short conversation with the Marquise's mother, bowed at once to the company and withdrew to his room, they were all once more left standing there, and were at a loss to know what to think. The commandant expressed the opinion that the matter should be allowed to take its course. He was in all probability counting on his relatives. The Count would otherwise be faced with dishonourable discharge. Frau von G** asked her daughter what she felt about him, and whether she might not be able to say something which might avoid a catastrophe. 'Dearest Mother,' the Marquise answered, 'that is not possible! I am sorry that my gratitude is being so sternly tested. But I have resolved not to marry again; I do not wish to chance my happiness, and certainly not so rashly, a second time.' The Forstmeister observed that if this was her firm intention, then such a declaration could also help the Count, and it did seem almost imperative that they should give him *some* definite answer. Frau von G** replied that since this young man, who had so many extraordinary qualities to recommend him, had declared his wish to settle in Italy, she believed that his offer merited some consideration, and that the Marquise's decision deserved to be reconsidered. The Forstmeister, sitting down by the Marquise's side, asked her whether she found the Count, as a person, pleasing. The Marquise replied, with some embarrassment, that she found him both attractive and unattractive; and appealed to the others for their opinion. Frau von G** said: 'When he returns from Naples, and if the enquiries we were to make in the meantime revealed nothing that contradicted the general impression you have formed of him, how would you react if he were to repeat his proposal?' 'In such a case,' said the Marquise, 'I would – since his wishes did seem so urgent –' she hesitated at this moment and her eyes shone – 'I would consent to these wishes, because of the obligation that I owe him.' Her mother, who had always wished her daughter to marry a second time, had difficulty in concealing her joy at this declaration, and turned her mind to the possible advantages. The Forstmeister, rising to his feet again with some disquiet, said that if there were even the faintest possibility of the Marquise giving her hand one day to the Count in marriage, immediate steps should now be taken to achieve this aim, in order to prevent the consequences of his reckless action. Frau von G** was of the same opinion and remarked that they would not, after all, be taking a very great risk, since the young man had displayed so many excellent qualities during that night when the Russians had attacked the fortress, that there was no reason to assume that he was not a person of irreproachable character. The Marquise lowered her gaze with an expression of great agitation. 'After all,' her mother continued, taking her by the hand, 'we could perhaps intimate to him that you will undertake not to enter into any other engagement, until he has returned from Naples.' '*That* undertaking, dearest Mother,' said the Marquise, 'I can indeed give him; I fear, however, that it will not satisfy him but will compromise us.' 'Let that be my concern!' replied her mother with great delight; and looked around for her husband. 'Lorenzo! What do you think?' she asked, and made a move to get to her feet. The commandant, who had heard everything, stood by the window, looked out onto the street, and said nothing. The Forstmeister declared that he would, on the strength of this non-committal assurance from her, undertake to get the Count out of the house. 'Then be quick about it, be quick about it!' exclaimed his father, turning round. 'That's twice I've had to surrender to this Russian!' At this his wife leapt to her feet, kissed him and their daughter and enquired, with a bustle which made her husband smile, how they were going to inform the Count of this decision without delay. It was decided, at the suggestion of the Forstmeister, to have a servant request him, if he were not already undressed, to be so good as to join the family for a moment. The Count responded by saying that he would at once have the honour to appear, and, hardly had the servant returned with this message, when he himself, with joy winging his steps, entered the room and, deeply moved, prostrated himself at the Marquise's feet. The commandant was about to speak, but the Count, standing up, declared that he already knew enough! He kissed the hands of the colonel and his wife, embraced the Marquise's brother, and merely asked if they would do him the favour of helping him procure a coach as quickly as possible. The Marquise, although moved by this scene, said: 'I hope, Count, that you will not harbour any rash hopes –' 'By no means, by no means!' replied the Count. 'No harm will have been done, if the enquiries that you make about me turn out not to contradict those emotions which have just caused you to recall me to your presence.' Whereupon the commandant embraced him heartily, the Forstmeister immediately offered him his own carriage, a groom sped to the post-station to order horses at a premium rate, and the whole departure was characterised by more pleasure than has ever attended a guest's arrival. The Count expressed the hope that he would be able to overtake his dispatches in B**, from where he now intended to set out for Naples by a shorter route than the one through M**; in Naples he would do his utmost to cancel the further assignment to Constantinople; and since he was resolved, if need be, to report himself sick, he could guarantee that, unless prevented by unavoidable circumstances, he would without fail be back again in M** within four to six weeks. At this moment his groom announced that the carriage was harnessed and everything ready for his departure. The Count picked up his hat, went up to the Marquise, and took her hand. 'Well, then, Julietta,' he said, 'I am now at least to some extent reassured.' He laid his hand in hers and added: 'And yet I had longed for us to be married before I left.' 'Married!' exclaimed the whole family. 'Married,' repeated the Count, kissed the hand of the Marquise whom he assured, when she asked whether he had taken leave of his senses, that she would one day understand what he meant! The family was on the point of getting angry with him, but he immediately bade them all farewell with great warmth, asked them to think no further about his last remark, and departed.

Several weeks passed, during which the whole family, with very different feelings, awaited the outcome of this strange affair. The commandant received a courteous letter from General K**, the Count's uncle; the Count himself wrote from Naples; the enquiries that had been made about him turned out to be rather favourable; in short, the engagement was regarded as virtually sealed – when the Marquise's ailments returned, more acutely than ever before. She noticed a baffling change in her figure. She unburdened herself with great frankness to her mother, and confessed that she did not know what to make of her condition. Such strange symptoms caused her mother to become extremely concerned about her daughter's health, and she insisted that she should consult a doctor. The Marquise, hoping to recover by virtue of her natural good health, resisted; she suffered severely for several more days without following her mother's advice, until, experiencing over and over again sensations of the most bizarre kind, she was thrown into a state of most acute anxiety. She sent for a doctor who enjoyed her father's trust, invited him, when her mother had just gone out for a moment, to sit down on the divan, and jestingly told him, after a few introductory remarks, what condition she believed herself to be in. The doctor gave her a searching look and, having carried out a careful examination, was silent for a while, before replying with a most grave expression that the Marquise's assessment was correct. When the lady enquired what exactly he meant, he explained himself with great clarity and said, with a smile he could not suppress, that she was perfectly healthy and did not need a doctor, whereupon the Marquise rang the bell, shot him a very severe sidelong glance, and asked him to leave. She murmured beneath her breath, as though he were not worthy of being addressed personally, that she had no inclination to joke with him about such matters. The doctor, offended, replied that he could only wish that she had always been so little inclined to jest as she was now; picked up his stick and hat, and prepared to depart at once. The Marquise assured him that she would inform her father of his insults. The doctor replied that he would stand by his statement in any court of law, proceeded to open the door, bowed and prepared to leave the room. As he paused to pick up a glove he had dropped, the Marquise asked how such a thing could be possible. The doctor replied that it was not his task to explain the facts of life to her, bowed to her once more and took his leave.

The Marquise stood there, as if thunderstruck. She pulled herself together and was on the point of rushing to her father; but the strangely grave demeanour of the doctor, by whom she felt so insulted, rooted her to the spot. She threw herself onto the divan in the greatest agitation. Mistrustful of herself, she ran through every moment of the past year, and came to the conclusion that she must be going mad when she thought of what she had just gone through. At last her mother appeared; and in answer to her alarmed enquiry as to why she was so distressed, the Marquise informed her of what the doctor had just said. Frau von G** branded him a shameless and contemptible good-for-nothing, and encouraged her daughter to report the insult to her father. The Marquise assured her that the doctor had been utterly serious and seemed determined to repeat his mad assertion to her father's face. Frau von G** then asked, not a little shocked, whether there was any possibility of her being in such a condition? 'I would sooner believe that graves can be made fertile,' answered the Marquise, 'and wombs of corpses give birth!' 'Come, come, you strange little thing,' said her mother, hugging her warmly, 'what can be worrying you, then? If your conscience is clear, what does a doctor's opinion matter, or indeed the opinion of a whole panel of doctors? Whether this particular doctor is mistaken or malicious, why should that concern you? Nonetheless, it is right that we should tell your father about it.' 'Oh God!' said the Marquise, with a convulsive quiver, 'how can I set my mind at rest? Do not my own feelings, those innermost feelings I know all too well, speak against me? Would I not, if I knew that another woman was feeling as I do, would I not come to the same conclusion – that this is indeed the truth of the matter?' 'This is terrible!' exclaimed her mother. 'Malicious! Mistaken!' continued the Marquise. 'What reasons can that man, whom we have always respected until today, possibly have for insulting me so wilfully and despicably? Why, when I have never offended him, when

I received him here with complete trust, sensing that I would in future be grateful to him; when he came to me with the genuine wish, as his very first words demonstrated, to help me, rather than cause more searing pain than I was already suffering? And if I were compelled,' she continued, while her mother gazed at her unflinchingly, 'to choose between the two possibilities, and came to the conclusion that he had made a mistake, is it at all possible that a doctor, even if he were only moderately skilful, could be mistaken in such a case?' Her mother replied, a little mischievously, that it had, of necessity, to be one or the other. 'Yes, dearest Mother!' answered the Marquise, kissing her hand with an expression of offended dignity, and blushing crimson, 'that is true! But the circumstances are so extraordinary that I may be permitted to doubt it. I swear, since it seems that some assurance is needed, that my conscience is as clear as that of my own children; even your own, dear and respected Mother, cannot be clearer. Nonetheless, I would ask you to send for a midwife, so that I might convince myself of the truth, and, whatever that truth may be, set my mind at rest.' 'A midwife!' exclaimed Frau von G** indignantly. 'A clear conscience and a midwife!' And speech failed her. 'A midwife, my dearest mother,' repeated the Marquise, falling on her knees in front of her, 'and forthwith, if I am not to go out of my mind.' 'Oh, with pleasure,' replied the commandant's wife, 'but the confinement shall not, if you please, take place in my house.' And with that she stood up and was about to leave the room. The Marquise, following her with outstretched arms, fell headlong onto the floor, and clasped her knees. 'If my irreproachable life,' she cried with the eloquence born of anguish, 'a life modelled on yours, gives me any claim to your respect, if your heart harbours for me any maternal feelings at all, even if only for so long as my guilt is

24

not yet proved and crystal clear, then do not abandon me at this horrific time.' 'But what is upsetting you?' asked her mother. 'Is it nothing more than your doctor's verdict? Nothing more than your innermost feelings?' 'Nothing more, dear Mother,' replied the Marquise, and laid her hand upon her breast. 'Nothing, Julietta?' continued her mother. 'Think carefully. An indiscretion, though that would cause me indescribable pain, would be forgivable and I should in the end have to forgive it; but if, in order to avoid a mother's censure, you were to invent a fantasy about the overturning of the world order, and were to reiterate blasphemous vows in order to convince my heart, which is all too eager to believe you – that would be shameful; I could never love you again after that.' 'May the gates of salvation one day be as open to me as my soul is now open to you,' cried the Marquise. 'I have concealed nothing from you, Mother.' This declaration, uttered with great emotion, affected her mother deeply. 'Oh Heaven above!' she cried, 'my dear child! How you move me!' And she lifted her up, and kissed her, and pressed her to her heart. 'Then what on earth are you afraid of? Come, you are very sick.' She tried to put her to bed, but the Marquise, weeping copiously, assured her that she was quite well, and that there was nothing at all wrong with her, apart from her strange and incomprehensible condition. 'Condition!' exclaimed her mother once more. 'What condition? If your recollection of the past is so clear, what insane apprehension has possessed you? Is it not possible that such inner feelings, which operate only obscurely, can deceive one?' 'No, no!' said the Marquise, 'they do not deceive me! And if you will be good enough to call the midwife, she will tell you that this terrible, destructive thing is true.' 'Come, my darling,' said Frau von G**, who was beginning to fear for her daughter's sanity.

'Come, come with me, and lie down in bed. What was it you thought the doctor said? Your face is burning so! You're trembling all over! Now, what was it the doctor said?' And no longer believing the scene her daughter had described to her, she tried to lead her away. The Marquise smiled through her tears and said: 'My dear, wonderful mother! I am in full possession of my senses. The doctor told me that I am expecting a child. Send for the midwife – and as soon as she tells me that it is not true, I shall be calm once more.' 'All right, all right!' replied the commandant's wife, suppressing her apprehension. 'Let her come at once, if you wish her to make a fool of you and tell you what a silly girl you are to dream up such things; let her come at once.' And so saying, she rang the bell and immediately sent one of her servants to summon the midwife.

When the midwife arrived the Marquise was still lying, with heaving breast, in the embrace of her mother who told the woman about the strange fancy with which her daughter was afflicted. The Marquise, she explained, swore that she had behaved virtuously, and yet deemed it necessary, deceived by some inexplicable feeling, for a professional expert to examine her condition. The midwife, while she carried out her examination, spoke of hot-blooded youth and the cunning ways of the world; and remarked, having completed her task, that she had encountered such cases before: young widows who found themselves in the same position all claimed to have lived on deserted islands; comforted the Marquise and assured her that the flamboyant corsair, who had come ashore at the dead of night, would in due course be found. At these words, the Marquise fainted. Her mother, who could not suppress her maternal affection, managed, with the midwife's help, to revive her, but was overwhelmed by indignation as soon as her daughter came to her senses. 'Julietta!' she cried with the keenest anguish. 'Will you confess to me, will you name the father?' – and yet still seemed disposed to reconciliation. But when the Marquise replied that she would go mad, her mother rose from the divan and said: 'Go, get out of my sight, you despicable creature! I curse the hour I bore you!' And left the room.

The Marquise, who was about to lose consciousness once more, drew the midwife down in front of her and, trembling violently, laid her head against her breast. With a faltering voice, she asked her about the ways of nature, and whether it was possible to conceive a child unwittingly. The midwife smiled, loosened her shawl and said that in her ladyship's case that would surely not be so. The Marquise answered that, no, no, she had conceived knowingly; she was merely curious in a general way to know whether there was such a phenomenon in the realm of nature. The midwife replied that, with the exception of the Blessed Virgin, such a thing had never yet happened to any woman on earth. The Marquise trembled more violently. She felt she was going to give birth at any moment and, clinging to the midwife in convulsive fear, begged her not to leave her. The midwife calmed her down. She assured her that her confinement was still a considerable way off, told her of ways in which it was possible in such cases to avoid malicious gossip, and said that everything would turn out nicely. But as these consoling remarks merely pierced the unhappy lady's heart, the Marquise pulled herself together, announced that she was feeling better, and requested her attendant to leave.

The midwife had hardly left the room when a servant brought the Marquise a note from her mother in which she wrote:

Herr von G** wishes you, in view of the present circum-
stances, to leave his house. He encloses the papers relating
to your fortune, and hopes that God will spare him the grief
of ever setting eyes on you again.

The letter was by now wet with tears, and in one corner stood
the smudged word: 'dictated'. Tears of grief flooded from the
Marquise's eyes. Weeping bitterly over her parents' error, and
the injustice into which these excellent people had been
deludedly led, she went to her mother's quarters. She was
told that her mother was with the commandant; and she made
her way there with faltering steps. When she found the door
locked, she fell to the floor, and invoked all the saints to
witness her innocence. She must have been lying there for
a few minutes when the Forstmeister emerged and, with his
face flaming with anger, said that she was well aware that
her father did not wish to see her. The Marquise, sobbing
uncontrollably, exclaimed: 'Dearest brother!'; and forcing her
way into the room, cried: 'Beloved Father!' and held out her
arms towards him. As soon as he saw her, the commandant
turned his back on her and hurried to his bedroom. And when
she followed him there, he shouted: 'Get out!' and tried
to slam the door; but when she, moaning and pleading,
prevented him from doing so, he suddenly relented and,
letting the Marquise into the room, crossed to the far wall. As
he had turned his back on her, she flung herself at his feet and,
trembling, clasped his knees, at which point the pistol he had
seized went off, just as he was fetching it from the wall, and
a bullet smashed into the ceiling. 'Lord have mercy on me!'
exclaimed the Marquise, rose to her feet as pale as death and
hurried away from her father's apartment. She ordered the
horses to be harnessed at once, entered her own apartment,

slumped exhausted into a chair, swiftly dressed her children, and had all her belongings packed. She was just wrapping one more garment round her youngest child, whom she was holding between her knees, and was about to climb into the carriage, now that everything was ready for departure – when the Forstmeister entered and ordered her, on the commandant's behalf, to hand over her children and leave them behind. 'My children!' she exclaimed and rose to her feet. 'Tell your inhuman father that he may come and gun me down, but not tear my children from me!' And fortified with all the pride of innocence, she snatched up her children, carried them into the coach and, without her brother daring to stop her, drove off.

With the self-knowledge gained through this beautiful exertion, she suddenly raised herself, as though by her own hands, from the depths into which fate had cast her. The turmoil, that was tearing her heart in two, now subsided when she found herself out in the open; she covered her children, these little treasures, with kisses, and reflected with great satisfaction on the victory she had won over her brother by virtue of her guilt-free conscience. Her reason, strong enough not to give way under the pressure of her strange situation, submitted itself entirely to the great, sacred and inexplicable order of the world. She realised the impossibility of ever convincing her family of her innocence, understood that, if she were not to go under, she must come to terms with this fact – and only a few days had elapsed after her arrival in V**, when her grief gave way to a heroic resolve to arm herself with pride against the slings of fortune. She decided to withdraw utterly into herself and dedicate herself zealously and exclusively to the education of her two children, and to attend with full maternal love and care to the gift that God had bestowed on her in the shape of the third child. Due to her long absence, her beautiful country house had fallen into some disrepair, and she now made arrangements to have it restored in a few weeks' time, when her confinement would be over; and sat in the summer-house, knitting little caps and stockings for little feet, and thinking about how she could best make use of the various rooms – which, for example, she would fill with books, and which might most easily accommodate her easel. And thus it was that before the date of Count F**'s expected return from Naples had passed, she had completely accepted her fate of leading a life of perpetual convent-like seclusion. Her porter was ordered to let no visitors into the house. The only unbearable thought was that the little creature, which she had conceived in the utmost innocence and purity, and whose origin, precisely because it was more mysterious, also seemed more sacred than that of other human beings, was destined to be branded a disgrace in good society. An unusual stratagem for discovering the father had occurred to her: a stratagem which, when she first thought of it, caused her to drop her knitting with fright. Restless and sleepless, and for whole nights on end, she turned it over and over in her mind in an attempt to get used to the idea which, by its very nature, offended her innermost feeling. She still resisted the idea of entering into any relationship with the person who had deceived her in such a fashion; for she quite correctly drew the conclusion that he must belong, irredeemably, to the very scum of the earth, and that, whatever his place in the world, he could only have issued from its basest, vilest filth. But since her sense of independence grew ever stronger within her, and she reflected that a precious stone retains its value however it may be set, she plucked up courage one morning, as she felt new life stirring inside her, and had that extraordinary announcement, quoted to the reader at the beginning of this story, printed in the M** news-sheets.

Count F**, meanwhile, detained in Naples by unavoidable duties, had written to the Marquise for a second time, urgently requesting her that, should unusual circumstances arise, it would be advisable for her to abide by the tacit undertaking she had given him. As soon as he had succeeded in putting off another business journey to Constantinople, and as soon as his other plans permitted it, he left Naples and arrived in M** only a few days later than the date he had given. The commandant received him with an embarrassed expression, said he had to leave the house on unavoidable business, and asked the Forstmeister to entertain him instead. The Forstmeister took him to his room and asked him, after a brief greeting, whether he already knew what had happened in his absence at the commandant's house. The Count, turning pale for a second, answered: 'No.' The Forstmeister then informed him of the disgrace which the Marquise had brought upon the family, and told him everything that our readers have just discovered. The Count struck his forehead with his hand. 'Why are so many obstacles put in my way!' he exclaimed, forgetting himself. 'If the marriage had taken place, we should have been spared all this shame and unhappiness!' The Forstmeister, staring at him in amazement, asked whether he were insane enough to wish to be married to such a worthless creature. The Count replied that she was worth more than the entire world which despised her, that he believed implicitly her protestations of innocence; and that he intended to go that very day to V** and repeat to her his offer. And he quickly picked up his hat, bade farewell to the Forstmeister, who thought he had taken leave of his senses, and left.

He mounted his horse and galloped out to V**. Having

dismounted at the gate, he was about to enter the forecourt, when the porter told him that the Frau Marquise wished to speak to no one. The Count enquired whether these instructions, designed for strangers, also applied to a friend of the house; whereupon the porter answered that he was aware of no exception, and then almost immediately enquired, in an ambiguous manner, whether he were not perhaps Count F**? The Count gave him a searching look and answered that he was not; then turning to his servant, said, in a loud enough voice for the other man to hear, that in those circumstances he would find accommodation at an inn and announce his presence to the Marquise in writing. As soon as he was out of the porter's sight, he sidled round the wall of an extensive garden that lay behind the house. He stepped into the garden by a door which he found unlocked, wandered along its avenues, and was just about to ascend the terrace to the rear of the house when, in an arbour to one side of it, he caught sight of the Marquise's charming and mysterious figure, as she sat busily working at a little table. He drew near to her in such a way that she only noticed him when he was standing at the entrance of the arbour, three small steps from her feet. 'Count F**!' cried the Marquise, as she looked up, and blushed crimson with surprise. The Count smiled, stood motionless in the entrance for a while; then, without frightening her by being too forward, sat down by her side and put his arm gently round her lovely waist, before she could decide what to do in so strange a situation. 'But Count, where can you possibly have come from?' asked the Marquise – and shyly lowered her gaze. 'From M**,' the Count replied, pressing her very gently to him. 'I found the back gate open. I felt that I could rely on your forgiveness, and walked in.' 'Did they not tell you in M**?' she asked, still motionless in his arms. 'Everything, dear lady,' replied the Count. 'But fully convinced of your innocence –' 'What!' cried the Marquise, rising to her feet, and freeing herself from his embrace, 'and yet you still come here?' 'Despite the world,' he continued, holding her close, 'and despite your family, and even despite this charming apparition' – at which he pressed an ardent kiss on her breast. 'Get out of my sight!' she exclaimed. 'So convinced am I of your innocence, Julietta, it's as though I were omniscient, as though my own soul dwelt in your body.' The Marquise cried, 'Let me go!' 'I have come,' he concluded – and still did not let her go – 'to repeat my proposal and to receive, if you accept it, the fortune of the blessed from your hand.' 'Let me go at once!' she cried, 'I order you to let me go!' and breaking free from his embrace, she drew away from him. 'Sweet, adorable creature!' he whispered, rising to his feet again and following her. 'You heard what I said!' cried the Marquise, turning away and evading him. 'A single, secret, whispered word!' said the Count, hastily reaching for her smooth arm as it slipped away from him. 'I *do not wish*,' she retorted, 'to hear a single word,' and pushing him violently away, she ran to the terrace and disappeared.

He had already climbed halfway up the terrace, determined at all costs that she should hear him out, when the door was slammed in his face and, as he approached, the bolt pushed home with distracted vehemence. He stood still for a moment, unsure of what he should do in such a situation, and weighed up whether he should climb in through an open side window, and pursue his purpose until he had achieved it; but however difficult, in every sense, it was for him to desist, it now seemed necessary to do so, and bitterly annoyed with himself that he had let her slip from his grasp, he slowly descended the terrace, left the garden and went to find his horses. He felt that his attempt to declare his feelings to her in person had irrevocably failed, and rode slowly back to M**, thinking about the letter he was now condemned to write. That evening, eating his supper in a foul mood at a crowded table, he met the Forstmeister, who immediately asked him whether his proposal in V** had been successfully concluded. The Count replied with a curt 'No!' and felt very much inclined to dispatch him with some bitter remark; but for the sake of politeness, he added after a while that he had resolved to write the lady a letter which would soon clarify the issue. The Forstmeister said he noticed with regret that the Count's passion for the Marquise was robbing him of his senses; he felt it his duty, however, to assure the Count that she was already in the process of making a different choice; and he rang for the latest newspapers and handed him the sheet which contained the Marquise's advertisement for the child's father. The Count flushed as his eyes ran over the text. He was filled with conflicting emotions. The Forstmeister enquired whether he thought the Marquise would succeed in finding the person in question. 'Undoubtedly!' replied the Count, as he pored over the article, greedily devouring its meaning. Then, having folded the newspaper and moved for a moment to the window, he said: 'All is now well! Now I know what I must do!' He turned quickly round, and, having politely asked the Forstmeister whether they would have the pleasure of meeting again soon, he took his leave and departed, wholly reconciled to his fate.

The commandant's house, meanwhile, had witnessed the liveliest of scenes. Frau von G** was incensed at her husband's destructive violence and at her own weakness in allowing him to override her objections to the tyrannical way in which he had banished their daughter. Although she had fainted when the pistol-shot rang out in his bedroom, from which her daughter had dashed, she recovered soon enough; but all the commandant did, when she came to, was apologise for causing her this unnecessary alarm, and throw the discharged pistol onto a table. Later, when he had asked the Marquise to hand over her children, she timidly ventured to say that he had no right to take such a step; she requested him, in a touching voice that was still faint from her recent swoon, to avoid violent scenes in the house; but the commandant's sole response was to turn, foaming with rage, to the Forstmeister and say: 'Go and get them!' When Count F**'s second letter arrived, the commandant had given orders for it to be sent to V**, where the Marquise was living, who, as the messenger later reported, had simply laid it to one side, saying that that would be all. Frau von G**, who was in the dark about so much in this whole affair, especially her daughter's inclination to get married again to a man for whom she felt nothing, tried in vain to introduce a discussion on this point. Each time she did so, the commandant asked her to be silent in a tone that resembled an order; and on one occasion he took down a portrait of his daughter that was still hanging on the wall, declaring that he wished to efface her from his memory, and that he no longer had a daughter. Then the Marquise's strange announcement was published in the papers. Her mother, who had been handed the paper by the commandant and had read it with absolute amazement, went with it to her husband's study, where she found him working at a table, and asked him what on earth he thought of it. The commandant continued writing and said: 'Oh, she is innocent!' 'What!' exclaimed Frau von G**, astonished beyond all measure, 'innocent?' 'She did it in her sleep,' said the commandant, without looking up. 'In her sleep!'

replied his wife. 'Do you mean to tell me that something so monstrous –' 'You fool!' exclaimed the commandant, gathered his papers up and left the room.

On the day when the newspaper was next published, Frau G**, sitting at breakfast with her husband, was perusing the news-sheet that had just arrived fresh from the press, and read the following answer:

> *If the Frau Marquise von O** will be present at eleven o'clock on the morning of the 3rd of ** in the house of her father Herr von G**, the man whom she seeks will be there to prostrate himself at her feet.*

Frau von G** fell silent before she had even read half of this extraordinary reply; she skimmed through to the end, and passed the sheet to the commandant. The colonel read it through three times, as if he could not believe his own eyes. 'Now tell me, Lorenzo, in Heaven's name, what do you make of that?' 'Oh, the infamous woman!' replied the commandant, getting up from the table, 'oh, the sly hypocrite! The lewdness of a bitch, coupled with the cunning of a fox and multiplied ten times over – that is nothing to what she is. Such a face! Such eyes! More innocent than a cherub's!' And nothing could calm him in his grief. 'But if it is trick,' asked his wife, 'what on earth does she hope to achieve?' 'Achieve?' retorted the colonel, 'she is determined, come what may, to deceive us with her contemptible cunning. She and that man have already learnt by heart their little tale, which they will burden us with when they appear here on the third at eleven in the morning. And I shall be expected to say: "My darling daughter, I had no idea, who could have thought such a thing, forgive me, receive my blessing and let us be friends again." But a bullet awaits the man who crosses my threshold on the third! Or perhaps it would be more fitting to have him thrown out of the house by the servants.' Frau von G**, after a further perusal of the announcement in the paper, said that, if she were forced to believe one of two incomprehensible things, she would sooner believe in an unheard-of twist of fate than such a despicable act perpetrated by her daughter who had always been so virtuous. But even before she had finished speaking, the commandant was already shouting: 'Kindly oblige me and hold your tongue!' And added, as he left the room: 'I hate to hear the matter mentioned even.'

A few days later the commandant received a letter from the Marquise referring to the second announcement in which she begged him, most respectfully and touchingly, since she had been deprived of the privilege of setting foot in his house, kindly to send whoever presented himself there on the morning of the third to her on her estate at V**. Frau von G** chanced to be present when the commandant received this letter, and the expression on his face clearly told her that his feelings had become confused; for if it were a trick, what possible motive could she now have, since she appeared to be making no attempt to gain his pardon? Emboldened by this, she devised a plan which she had long carried in her heart, and which had been beset by doubts. As the General still stared impassively at the paper, she announced that she had an idea. Would he permit her to go for a few days out to V**? She would succeed in getting the Marquise, if she really did know the man who had answered her advertisement as a stranger, to betray herself, even if she were the most cunning of deceivers. The commandant, tearing the letter to shreds in a sudden fit of violence, replied that she knew full well that he wished to have nothing at all to do with his daughter, and forbade his wife from communicating with her in any way at all. He sealed the shredded letter in an envelope, wrote the Marquise's address on it and returned it to the messenger as his sole reply. Frau von G**, secretly exasperated by this stubbornness which would destroy any possibility of clearing the matter up, resolved to carry out her plan without her husband's permission. On the very next morning, when her husband was still lying in bed, she drove out to V**, accompanied by one of his grooms. When she arrived at the gate of her estate, the porter told her that nobody was to be admitted to the Marquise. Frau von G** replied that she was already aware of these orders, but that he should now go and announce the wife of Colonel G**. To which the man replied that this would achieve nothing, since the Frau Marquise would speak to not a single soul. Frau von G** replied that she would be received, since she was her mother; would he kindly, therefore, delay no further and do as he was bidden. But hardly had the porter, still believing that his mission would be fruitless, entered the house, than the Marquise was seen to emerge from it, hasten to the gate, and fall to her knees before her mother's carriage. Frau von G**, assisted by her groom, dismounted, and in some commotion, lifted the Marquise from the ground. Overcome by her own feelings, the Marquise bowed low to kiss her mother's hand; then, shedding frequent tears, she led her with great deference through the rooms of her house. 'My dearest mother!' she cried, having seated her on a divan; she stood in front of her and, drying her eyes, said: 'To what happy chance do I owe the priceless pleasure of seeing you?' Frau von G** hugged her daughter and said that she simply wished to apologise for the brutal way in which she had been expelled from her parents' house. 'Apologise!' cried the Marquise, and tried to kiss her hand. But her mother, avoiding the kiss, continued: 'Not only did the recently published answer to your advertisement convince both your father and me of your innocence, but I also have to tell you that yesterday, to our great and joyous astonishment, he presented himself at our house.' '*Who?*' asked the Marquise, and sat down at her mother's side. '*Who* presented himself?' And her face grew tense with expectation. 'He,' replied Frau von G**, 'the man who wrote that reply, the very man to whom your appeal was directed.' 'Well, then,' said the Marquise, her breast heaving with apprehension, 'who is he?' And she repeated: 'Who is he?' 'That,' replied Frau von G**, 'is what I would like you to guess. For just imagine – yesterday, as we were having tea, reading that extraordinary newspaper announce-ment, a man with whom we are very closely acquainted, rushed into the room with gestures of despair and prostrated himself first at your father's and then at my feet. We, not knowing what to make of all this, asked him to explain. He replied that his conscience would give him no peace, that it was he who had shamefully deceived the Frau Marquise, that he simply had to know how his crime was judged, and that if retribution were to be exacted, he had come to take his punishment.' 'But who? who? who?' asked the Marquise. 'As I was saying,' continued Frau von G**, 'an otherwise well brought-up young man, whom we should never have thought capable of such a base act. But you must not be alarmed, my daughter, to hear that he is of low birth and that he lacks all the requirements that a husband of yours might otherwise be expected to have.' 'Nevertheless, my most excellent mother,' said the Marquise, 'he cannot be wholly unworthy, since he came to throw himself at your feet, before throwing himself at mine. But who? Who? Just tell me who!' 'Well,' replied her mother, 'it was Leopardo, the Tyrolese hunter whom your father recently engaged and whom, as you may have noticed, I have brought with me to present to you as your fiancé.' 'Leopardo, the hunter!' cried the Marquise, pressing her hand to her brow in a gesture of despair. 'Why are you amazed?' asked her mother. 'Have you reasons for doubting it?' 'How? Where? When?' asked the Marquise in confusion. 'That,' answered her mother, 'is something he wishes to confide to you alone. Shame and love made it impossible, he said, to explain such things to anyone else but you. But if you like, we will open the ante-room where he, with beating heart, is waiting for the outcome; and you shall see, while I leave you alone, whether you can worm his secret out of him.' 'Oh God in heaven!' cried the Marquise: 'I remember how I once fell asleep in the midday heat and, on waking, saw him walk away from the divan!' She blushed crimson with shame and covered her face with her little hands. But as the Marquise spoke these words, her mother fell to her knees before her. 'Oh my daughter!' she exclaimed; 'Oh you exemplary girl!' And she folded her daughter in her arms. 'How contemptible of me!' she went on, and buried her face in her daughter's lap. 'What is the matter, Mother?' the Marquise asked in consternation. 'Let me tell you, you who are purer than any angel, that nothing I have been saying is true, that my corrupted soul could not believe in the great innocence that glows around you, and that I could only convince myself of it by descending to this shameful cunning.' 'My dearest mother!' cried the Marquise and bent down full of happiness to raise her to her feet. But her mother said: 'I shall not move from your feet, you wonderful, ethereal creature, until you tell me that you can forgive my despicable behaviour.' 'I am to forgive you?! Oh, dearest Mother, stand up, I beg you.' 'You heard me,' said Frau von G**, 'I want to know whether you can still love me and still respect me as before.' 'My adored mother!' cried the Marquise, and likewise fell to her knees; 'love and respect have never left my heart. Who, under such extraordinary circumstances, could possibly trust me? How happy I am that you are convinced of my blamelessness!' 'My dearest child,' said Frau von G**, standing up with her daughter's assistance, 'I shall now overwhelm you with care and attention. You shall have your confinement in my house; and I shall treat you with as much tenderness and respect as would be the case if you were to give birth to a young prince. I shall never desert you for as long as I live. I defy the whole world; I *want* no greater honour than your shame – provided you will love me again and forget the brutal way I banished you.' The Marquise tried to comfort her with endless caresses and entreaties, but evening fell and midnight struck before she had succeeded. Next day, when the old lady had recovered a little from her emotion, which had brought on a high fever during the night, mother, daughter and grandchildren drove back, as if in triumph, to M**. Their journey could not have been happier, they joked about the hunter Leopardo, as he sat on the carriage-box in front of them; and the Marquise's mother said she noticed how her daughter blushed whenever she looked at his broad shoulders, and the Marquise answered, partly with a sigh and partly with a smile: 'And yet I wonder who the man will be who comes to our house on the morning of the third!' But as they approached M**, their mood grew more serious again, in anticipation of the momentous scenes that awaited them. Frau von G**, who revealed nothing of her plans, led her daughter, when they had both dismounted from the carriage, back to her old rooms, told her to make herself comfortable and then, saying she would soon be back, slipped away. She returned after an hour with her face very flushed.

'Would you believe it! What a doubting Thomas!' she said, with secret delight, 'what a doubting Thomas! Sixty whole minutes I needed to convince him! But now he sits there weeping.' 'Who?' asked the Marquise. 'He,' answered her mother. 'Who else but the person with the most cause!' 'Surely not my father?' exclaimed the Marquise. 'Like a child,' replied her mother, 'and if I had not had to wipe the tears from my own eyes, I would have laughed as soon as I had left the room and closed the door.' 'And all that because of me?' asked the Marquise, rising to her feet, 'and I am supposed to stay here?–' 'Stay where you are!' said Frau von G**. 'Why did he dictate that letter to me! He shall come to *you*, if he ever wishes to see *me* again!' 'My dearest mother,' pleaded the Marquise, but her mother interrupted her. 'I shall not relent. Why did he reach for the pistol?' 'But I beseech you –' 'You *shall* not go to him!' replied Frau von G**, forcing her daughter to sit down again. 'And if he doesn't come by this evening, I shall leave with you tomorrow.' The Marquise described this behaviour as hard and unfair. But her mother replied: 'Calm yourself' – for she could already hear someone sobbing along the corridor – 'he's already here!' 'Where?' asked the Marquise, and listened. 'Is someone outside the door? What is that convulsive –' 'Of course!' replied Frau von G**. 'He wants us to open the door for him.' 'Let me go!' cried the Marquise, and jumped up from the chair. 'No, Julietta, if you love me, stay where you are,' said her mother; and at that moment the commandant entered the room, holding a handkerchief to his face. Frau von G** placed herself directly between him and her daughter, and turned her back on her husband. 'My dearest father!' cried the Marquise, and stretched out her arms towards him. 'Just stay where you are, do you hear!' said her mother. The commandant stood there in the room, weeping.

'He must apologise to you,' continued Frau von G**. 'Why has he such a temper, and why is he so stubborn! I love him, but I love you too. And if I have to make a choice, then you are a finer person than he, and I shall stay with you.' The commandant was bent double, and wept so loudly that the walls echoed. 'My God!' cried the Marquise, suddenly giving in to her mother, and took out her handkerchief to let her own tears flow. Frau von G** said: 'It's just that he can't speak!' and moved a little to one side. At this the Marquise got to her feet, embraced the commandant and begged him to be calm. She was also weeping profusely. She asked him whether he would like to sit down, and tried to help him onto a chair; she pushed one towards him, but he didn't react, and could not be persuaded to move; neither did he sit down; he merely stood there, looked at the ground and wept. The Marquise, holding him upright, half turned to her mother and said that he would make himself ill; her mother also seemed on the verge of losing her composure, as she observed his convulsive movements. But when the commandant, yielding to his daughter's repeated pleas, finally sat down, and the Marquise, caressing him all the time, had sunk down at his feet, Frau von G**, returning to her theme, declared that it served him right and that he would now no doubt come to his senses; whereupon she withdrew and left the two of them alone in the room.

As soon as she was outside the door, she wiped away her own tears, wondering whether the violent distress she had caused him might after all be dangerous, and whether it would be advisable to send for a doctor. She cooked dinner for him in the kitchen, and prepared the most fortifying and comforting dishes that she could produce; she prepared and warmed his bed, intending to lay him down there as soon as, hand in hand with his daughter, he would appear; but when the dinner-table was laid and there was still no sign of him, she crept back to the Marquise's room to listen to what was going on. She put her ear gently to the door and heard the fading echo of some softly murmured words that had been uttered, it seemed to her, by the Marquise; and peering through the keyhole, she noticed that she was even sitting on the commandant's lap, something he had never once in his life permitted. And when finally she opened the door, she beheld a sight that made her heart leap with joy: her daughter was lying peacefully in her father's arms, with her head thrown back and her eyes shut tight, while he sat in his armchair and pressed long, ardent and avid kisses onto her mouth, just like a lover! His daughter said nothing, he said nothing; he sat with his face bowed over her, as though she were his first love, touched her lips with his fingers, and kissed her. Her mother felt she was in heaven; standing unseen behind his chair, she was loathe to interrupt the blissful scene of reconciliation that had restored happiness to her home. Finally, she drew near her husband and, leaning round the side of the chair, looked at him as he began once more to stroke and kiss his daughter's mouth with indescribable rapture. When the commandant saw her, he frowned, lowered his eyes again and was about to say something, when she exclaimed: 'What an extraordinary face!' It was now her turn to smooth out his face with kisses, after which she dispelled the emotional atmosphere through jesting. She summoned them both to dinner and they followed her, walking like a bridal couple, to table, where the commandant seemed very happy, despite intermittent sobs, ate and spoke little, gazed down at his plate and played with his daughter's hand.

It was now a question of who in the world would present himself at eleven o'clock on the following morning; for tomorrow was the dreaded third. The Marquise's parents and also her brother, who had arrived to take part in the general reconciliation, were decidedly in favour of marriage, if the man were even remotely acceptable; everything possible should now be done to ensure the Marquise's happiness. If, however, his circumstances turned out to be such that, even with the help of her family, they would fall far short of the Marquise's own, then her parents were opposed to the marriage; they would then be resolved to adopt the child and have the Marquise live with them as before. The Marquise, on the other hand, seemed prepared to keep her promise whatever the outcome – as long as the man in question was not a reprobate – and provide, at whatever cost, a father for the child. In the evening her mother raised the question of how the person was to be received. The commandant thought that, when eleven o'clock came, it would be most fitting to leave the Marquise alone. The Marquise, on the other hand, insisted that both her parents and her brother should be present, since she did not wish to share any secrets with the man. She also thought that this had seemed to be his own wish, as, in his answer, he had suggested her father's house as the meeting-place; and that was the reason, she added, why she had been greatly pleased by his answer. Her mother mentioned how unseemly, under such circumstances, the roles played by the Marquise's father and brother would be; she begged her daughter to agree that the two men should be absent, but was willing to accommodate her wishes by being present herself when the person arrived. After her daughter had thought it over for a while, this last proposal was finally accepted. Now at last, after a night of most stressful suspense, the morning of the dreaded third arrived. As the clock struck eleven, both women were sitting in the reception room, ceremonially attired as though for a betrothal, their hearts pounding so hard that they could have been heard, if the noises of day had ceased. The eleventh stroke was still ringing when Leopardo, the hunter whom the commandant had hired from the Tyrol, entered. 'Count F** has arrived, my lady, and wishes to be announced.' 'Count F**!' they both exclaimed at once, hurled from one kind of confusion to another. The Marquise cried: 'Lock the doors, we are not at home to him!' She rose at once to bolt the door of the room, and was about to drive out the groom who was standing in her way, when the Count, dressed in exactly the same uniform and with the same decorations and medals that he had worn on the day the fortress had been stormed, entered. The Marquise felt she would sink into the ground from sheer confusion; she reached for a handkerchief she had left lying on her chair, and was about to escape into a neighbouring room when her mother, seizing her by the hand, cried: 'Julietta!…' and fell silent, as though stifled by her thoughts. She stared straight at the Count and repeated, drawing her daughter towards her: 'Julietta! Come! Who else were we expecting?' The Marquise, whirling round, cried: 'Well? You surely can't mean him? –' and shot the Count a look that flashed like a thunderbolt, and her face turned deathly pale. The Count had gone down on one knee before her, his right hand placed on his heart, his head gently bowed, and there he remained, blushing crimson, looking down and saying nothing. 'Who else?' exclaimed Frau von G**, with a strangled voice, 'who else but him? How blind we have been!' The Marquise stood stiffly over him, and said: 'Mother, I shall go mad!' 'You foolish little thing!' replied her mother, and drew her towards her and whispered something in her ear. The Marquise turned away and, with both hands pressed against her face, sank onto the sofa. 'You poor wretched girl!'

her mother cried. 'What is wrong with you? What has taken you by surprise?' The Count did not move from Frau von G**'s side; he clasped, still kneeling, the outermost hem of her dress, and kissed it. 'Dear, gracious, most noble lady!' he whispered, and a tear rolled down his cheek. Frau von G** replied: 'Get to your feet, Count. If you can comfort her, we shall all be reconciled, and all shall be forgiven and forgotten.' The Count rose weeping to his feet. He knelt once more in front of the Marquise, he gently took her hand as if it were made of gold and the warmth of his own might tarnish it. But the Marquise, standing up, cried: 'Get out! get out! get out! I was prepared for a dissolute rake, but not – a devil!' moved away from him, as though he were infected with the plague, opened the door of the room and said: 'Call my father!' 'Julietta!' cried her mother in astonishment. The Marquise turned her wild, destructive looks onto the Count and then her mother; her breast heaved, her face blazed – no Fury's gaze could be more terrible. The commandant and the Forstmeister arrived. 'Father,' said the Marquise, as they were entering the room, 'I cannot marry this man!' And dipping her hand into a bowl of holy water fixed to the rear door, she scattered it in a wide arc over her father, mother and brother, and vanished.

The commandant, disturbed by this strange occurrence, asked what had happened; and turned pale when he noticed that Count F** was in the room at this decisive moment. His wife took the Count by the hand, and said: 'Ask no questions; this young man truly repents of all that has happened; give him your blessing, give it, give it – and all will still end happily.' The Count stood there utterly mortified. The commandant placed his hand on his shoulder; his eyelids quivered, his lips were as white as chalk. 'May you be spared the curse of

Heaven!' he exclaimed. 'When do you intend to marry?' 'Tomorrow,' answered Frau von G** for the Count, who was unable to utter a word, 'tomorrow or today, whichever you like; no time will be too soon for the Count, who has shown such admirable zeal in wishing to rectify his wrongdoing.' 'Then I shall have the pleasure of seeing you tomorrow at eleven o'clock in the Church of St Augustine!' said the commandant, bowed, called upon his wife and son to accompany him to the Marquise's room, and left the Count standing there.

They tried in vain to discover from the Marquise the reason for her strange behaviour; she lay in bed with a severe fever, refused to listen to any talk of marriage, and asked to be left alone. When asked why she had suddenly changed her mind and what made the Count more abhorrent to her than any other suitor, she looked at her father with a blank, wide-eyed expression and made no answer. Frau von G** asked whether she had forgotten that she was a mother, to which she replied that in this present case she had to think of herself more than her child, and reaffirmed, while invoking all the angels and saints as witnesses, that she would not marry. Her father, aware that she was in a hysterical state of mind, declared that she must keep her word, left her and, after an appropriate exchange of letters with the Count, had everything arranged for the marriage. He submitted to him a marriage contract by which he would forfeit all conjugal rights, while at the same time agreeing to fulfil any duties that might be required of him. The Count returned the document duly signed and covered in tears. When next morning the commandant handed it to the Marquise, she had recovered a little of her composure. Still sitting in bed, she read it through several times, folded it thoughtfully, opened it, and read it through once more;

she then declared that she would come to the Church of St Augustine at eleven o'clock. She got up, dressed without saying a word, and, when the hour struck, stepped into the carriage with the rest of her family and drove away.

The Count was not permitted to join the family until they had reached the entrance to the church. During the ceremony the Marquise stared with fixed gaze at the altarpiece; not even a fleeting glance did she bestow on the man with whom she was exchanging rings. When the marriage service was over, the Count offered her his arm; but as soon as they were outside the church once more, the Countess left with a bow; the commandant enquired whether he might have the honour of seeing him from time to time in his daughter's apartments, whereupon the Count muttered something unintelligible, raised his hat to those present and disappeared. He moved into apartments in M**, where he spent several months without once setting foot in the commandant's house, in which the Countess continued to live. It was only due to his sensitive, dignified and wholly exemplary behaviour whenever he came into contact with the family that, when the Countess was eventually delivered of an infant son, he was invited to the christening. The Countess, still confined and sitting in a bed with sumptuously embroidered coverlets, saw him only for an instant, as he entered and greeted her respectfully from afar. He threw onto the pile of presents, with which the other guests had welcomed the newborn boy and which lay on the child's cradle, two documents; when opened, after he had left, it turned out that one was a gift of twenty thousand roubles to the boy, and the other a will which made the boy's mother, in the event of the Count's death, heiress of his entire fortune. From that day on, Frau von G** saw to it that he was frequently invited; the house was open to him, and soon not an evening passed without him paying the family a visit. Since his instinct told him that, in consideration of the fragile nature of the world, they had all forgiven him, he now began to woo the Countess, his wife, once more; and after a year had passed she gave her consent for a second time, and a second wedding, happier than the first, was celebrated, after which the whole family settled on the estate at V**. A whole series of young Russians now followed the first; and when, during one happy hour, the Count asked his wife why, on that fateful third of the month, when she had seemed prepared to receive even the most dissolute rake, she had fled from him as if from a devil, she replied, throwing her arms around his neck, that he would not have appeared to her as a devil, if at their first meeting he had not seemed to her an angel.

The Earthquake in Chile

In Santiago, the capital of the kingdom of Chile, at the precise moment of the great earthquake of 1647, which cost many thousands of people their lives, a young Spaniard called Jerónimo Rugera, who had been accused of a criminal offence, was standing beside by a pillar of the prison, where he had been incarcerated, and was about to hang himself. About a year previously Don Enrico Asterón, one of the richest noblemen of the city, had turned him out of his house, where he had been employed as a tutor, because he had been on too intimate terms with Doña Josefa, his daughter. A secret assignation, to which the father had been alerted by the malicious vigilance of her proud brother, outraged the old man to such an extent, especially as he had expressly warned his daughter, that he sent her to the Carmelite convent of Our Dear Lady of the Mountain.

It was here, through happy chance, that Jerónimo had been able to resume the liaison and, during one discreet night, consummate his happiness in the convent garden. During the feast of Corpus Christi, when the solemn procession of nuns, with the novices behind, was just beginning, and the bells were pealing out, the hapless Josefa collapsed on the cathedral steps and went into labour.

This incident caused an extraordinary stir; the young sinner was immediately thrown into prison, without any regard for her condition, and no sooner was her confinement over than the archbishop commanded her to be put on trial with the utmost severity. This scandal was talked about in the town with such bitterness, and the whole convent, where it had taken place, criticised with such harshness, that neither the intercession of the Asterón family, nor even the wishes of the abbess herself, who had grown fond of the young girl because of her otherwise irreproachable conduct, were able to diminish the severity with which she was threatened by conventual law. All that happened was that the Viceroy, to the great indignation of the matrons and virgins of Santiago, commuted her sentence from death at the stake to death by beheading.

Windows were rented out and the rooves taken off the houses in the streets through which the execution procession was to pass, and the pious daughters of the city invited their girlfriends to witness with them this spectacle that was about to be offered to divine vengeance.

Jerónimo, who in the meantime had also been imprisoned, almost fainted when he was informed of this monstrous turn of events. In vain he pondered rescue plans: but wherever the wings of his most intrepid thoughts transported him, he came up against bolts and walls; and a foiled attempt to file through the window bars merely led to even stricter imprisonment. He prostrated himself before an image of the Holy Mother of God and prayed to her with infinite fervour, convinced that she alone could save him now.

Yet the dreaded day arrived, and with it an inner certainty of the utter hopelessness of his predicament. The bells that were to accompany Josefa to the place of execution began to toll, and he was overcome with despair. Hating his life, he decided to go to his death with the help of a rope that chance had left in his cell. He was standing, as already described, by a pillar, and was just fastening the rope, which he hoped would release him from this wretched world, to an iron bracket attached to the cornice, when suddenly, with a crash as if the firmament were falling in, the greater part of the city was swallowed up, and buried every living creature beneath its ruins. Jerónimo Rugera stood rigid with fear, and, as if all thoughts had been eradicated from his mind, he now clung to the pillar, on which he had wanted to die, and tried to stop himself falling. The ground was heaving beneath his feet, the walls of his prison cracked open, the whole edifice leaned over towards the street and would have crashed onto it, had not its own slow fall been shored up by the fall of the house opposite, the resulting arch, formed by chance, thus preventing its complete collapse. Trembling, his hair on end, his knees buckling beneath him, Jerónimo slid down the steeply sloping floor to the opening that had been torn in the façade of the prison, as the two buildings collided.

He was scarcely outside, when the whole of the already collapsing street was demolished by a second tremor. With no idea how to save himself from this general destruction, he clambered over wreckage and fallen timber, while death assailed him on every side, towards one of the nearest city gates. Here another house collapsed, and, hurling its debris in every direction, drove him into a side street; flames flashed through clouds of smoke, flickered from every gable and chased him terror-stricken into another street; here the Mapocho, having broken its banks, rolled roaring towards him and forced him into a third. Here lay a pile of corpses, there a voice still groaned beneath the rubble, here people were screaming from burning rooftops, there man and beast were struggling with the waves, here a courageous rescuer tried to help, and there stood another man, pale as death, stretching out his trembling hands to heaven. When Jerónimo had reached the gate and climbed a hill beyond it, he sank to the ground and fainted.

He must have lain there, deeply unconscious, for about fifteen minutes, before he finally came to and, with the city behind him, half raised himself up on the ground. He ran his hand over forehead and chest, not knowing what to make of his condition, and an indescribable feeling of bliss stole over him, as a westerly breeze from the sea fanned his reviving life, and his gaze wandered in all directions over the blossoming region of Santiago. The only thing to trouble him were crowds of distraught people, visible all around; he did not understand what could have brought them and him to this place, and only when he turned round and saw the city swallowed up beneath him did he recall the terrifying moment he had experienced. He bowed low and touched the ground with his brow to thank God for his miraculous escape; and as if this one horrific memory, etching itself on his mind, had obliterated all others, he wept with joy that life, in all its colourful wealth and variety, was still there for him to savour.

Then, noticing a ring on his finger, he suddenly remembered first Josefa, and then his prison, the tolling bells and the moment before the building collapsed. Deep sadness again filled his heart; he began to regret his prayer, and the Being who reigns above the clouds filled him with horror. He mingled with the people who, busily salvaging their possessions, were streaming out of the city gates, and ventured to enquire timidly about Asterón's daughter, and whether the sentence had been carried out – but no one could give him a detailed answer. A woman, bent almost double through carrying such an enormous load of household goods on her shoulders, and with two children clinging to her breast, said as she passed, as if she herself had been present, that Josefa had been beheaded. Jerónimo turned away; and since he himself, given the time that had passed, was also in no doubt that the execution had taken place, sat down in a lonely wood and abandoned himself to his grief. He wished that the destructive fury of nature would descend on him once more. He could not understand why he had escaped death, which his pitiful soul so craved, when that same death had, during those very moments, seemed of its own accord to offer him salvation on all sides. He was determined now not to flinch, even if the oak trees were to be uprooted and their crests come crashing down on top of him. Soon, when hope had come to him again in the midst of most bitter tears, and he had now finished weeping, he got to his feet and began to explore the area in every direction. He visited every hilltop on which people had gathered; he encountered streams of fugitives along every road; wherever a woman's dress fluttered in the breeze, he hastened trembling towards it; but the dress was never worn by his beloved Josefa. The sun was setting, and with it his hopes, when he reached the edge of a cliff which afforded him a view of a broad valley where only a few people had gathered. Unsure of what to do, he wandered from one group to another and was on the point of leaving them, when he suddenly noticed a young woman washing her child in the stream that ran through the ravine. And at this sight his heart pounded: full of foreboding, he leapt down from rock to rock, and with a cry of 'O Holy Mother of God!' recognised Josefa who looked round shyly on hearing him approach. With what rapture did the happy pair, saved by a divine miracle, embrace!

On the way to her death, Josefa had already come very close to the place of execution, when the buildings had suddenly begun to crash down, scattering to the four winds the procession that was leading her to the block. Her first horrified steps took her to the nearest gate of the town; but she came to her senses almost at once, turned round and rushed back to the convent where her small helpless son had been left behind. She found the whole convent ablaze; and the abbess who, during what were to have been her last moments, had promised to look after her baby, was standing at the entrance, crying out for help to rescue him. Fearlessly, Josefa dashed through the billowing smoke into the building that was already collapsing around her and, as if protected by all the angels of heaven, emerged once more at its gate, uninjured and with her child. She was just about to embrace the abbess, who had raised her hands in blessing over her head, when she and almost all her nuns, were struck dead by a falling gable in a most abominable way. Josefa recoiled trembling at this horrific sight; she hurriedly closed the abbess' eyes and fled, utterly terrified, to rescue her son, whom Heaven had restored to her, from the destruction.

She had only taken a few steps when she came across the dead body of the archbishop, which had just been dragged, mangled, from the rubble of the cathedral. The Viceroy's palace had collapsed, the law court, where she had been sentenced, was in flames, and where once her father's house had stood a lake had sprung up, boiling with reddish vapours. Josefa summoned her entire strength in order not to faint. Ignoring all the misery, she strode courageously on from street to street with her precious treasure, and was already near the gate when she saw the prison in ruins where Jerónimo had languished. The sight of this made her reel, and she all but fainted at the street corner when, at that very moment, a building whose foundations had been loosened by the tremors, crashed down behind her and drove her, panic-stricken, on; she kissed her child, wiped the tears from her eyes and, ignoring the horror that surrounded her, reached the gate. When she found herself in open country, she soon reached the conclusion that not everyone who had been inside a flattened building had necessarily been crushed.

She halted at the next crossroads and waited to see if the person whom, after Felipe, she loved more than anything in the world, might appear. Because no one came and the multitude of people increased, she continued on her way, and turned round again, and waited again; and then, shedding many tears, slipped into a dark pine-shaded valley to pray for his (as she believed) departed soul; and found him here, her lover, in the valley, and with him such bliss that the valley might have been the Garden of Eden.

All this she now told Jerónimo in a voice filled with emotion and gave him, when she had finished, the boy to kiss. Jerónimo took him and hugged him with the indescribable delight of fatherhood and, when the child cried at his unfamiliar face, covered him with endless kisses, until the child was silent. The loveliest of nights had meanwhile fallen with such mild fragrance, and so silvery and still, that only a poet could dream up such a scene. Everywhere along the banks of the stream people had settled in the glittering moonlight, and were preparing soft beds of moss and foliage on which to rest after such an agonising day. And because these wretched creatures were still lamenting, one the loss of his house, another that of his wife and child, and a third that of everything he owned, Jerónimo and Josefa moved quietly into thicker undergrowth, to avoid offending anyone by the secret exultation of their souls. They found a splendid pomegranate tree whose outstretched branches were laden with scented fruit, and on whose crest a nightingale warbled its voluptuous song. Jerónimo sat down against its trunk and, with Josefa on his lap and Felipe on hers, both covered by his cloak, they all rested. The tree's shadow, with its scattered light, passed over them, and the moon was already fading in the glow of dawn before they fell asleep – for there was no end to what they had to talk about, the convent garden, the prisons, and what they had both suffered for one another.

And how it moved them to think that so much misery had to be inflicted on the world that they might be happy!

They decided that, as soon as the tremors had ceased, they would go to La Concepción, where Josefa had a close friend and from where, with the small sum of money she hoped to borrow from her, they would be able to set sail for Spain, where Jerónimo's relatives on his mother's side lived, and where they could be happy until they died. At this point, amid many kisses, they fell asleep.

When they woke, the sun was already high in the sky, and they noticed several families nearby busy preparing themselves a small breakfast over a fire. Jerónimo was just thinking how he could get hold of some food for his own family, when a well-dressed young man, carrying an infant in his arms, approached Josefa and asked her with modesty whether she would be willing for a short time to suckle this poor little creature, whose mother was lying injured over there beneath the trees. Josefa was somewhat disconcerted when she recognised him as an acquaintance, but when, misinterpreting her confusion, he continued: 'It will only be for a few minutes, Doña Josefa, and the child has not been fed since the disaster caused us such suffering,' she said: 'I was silent for a different reason, Don Fernando; in terrible times like these, nobody refuses to share whatever they might have.' And with these words, she passed her own child to its father, took the little stranger and put it to her breast. Don Fernando was most grateful for this kindness, and asked whether she would like to join his own party, where breakfast was just being prepared at the fire. Josefa replied that she would accept the invitation with pleasure and followed him, as Jerónimo had no objections, to his family, where she received the most warm and affectionate welcome from his two sisters-in-law, whom she knew to be young ladies of most excellent character.

Doña Elvira, Don Fernando's wife, was lying on the ground with badly injured feet, and on seeing her gaunt little boy at Josefa's breast, she drew Josefa towards her with great affection. And Don Pedro, Elvira's father, who was wounded in the shoulder, also nodded tenderly in her direction.

Strange thoughts began to stir in Jerónimo and Josefa's minds. When they saw themselves treated with so much familiarity and kindness, they did not know what to think of the past, of the place of execution, the prison and the bells; or had they merely dreamt of all these things? It was as if, after the terrible blow which had shaken them all to the core, everyone was now reconciled. Their memories, it seemed, could reach no further back than the disaster. Only Doña Isabel, who had been invited by a friend to witness yesterday morning's spectacle but had declined the invitation, gazed dreamily from time to time at Josefa; but fresh reports of yet more horrific misfortunes snatched her thoughts back to the present, from which they had for a time strayed.

There were stories of how the town, immediately after the first main tremors, had teemed with women who had given birth to their children in full view of all the men; of how monks, crucifix in hand, had rushed to and fro, crying out that the end of the world had come; of how a guard, on the Viceroy's orders, had tried to clear a church of people, only to be told that there was no Viceroy of Chile any more; of how, in the worst moments of the earthquake, the Viceroy had been obliged to have gallows erected to put a stop to looting; and of how an innocent man, escaping a burning house through the back door, had been arrested by the over-zealous owner and lynched on the spot.

Doña Elvira, whose injuries Josefa was busily tending, had,

at a moment when these tales were being told with the utmost speed and excitement, taken the opportunity of asking her how she had fared on that terrible day. And when Josefa, with an oppressed heart, narrated some of the main details of her story, she was delighted to see this lady's eyes fill with tears. Doña Elvira seized her hand and pressed it, and bade her with a gesture to be silent. Josefa felt she was in the land of the blessed. She could not suppress the feeling that the previous day, despite all the wretchedness it had wreaked on the world, had been a boon such as Heaven had never before bestowed on it. And indeed, in the midst of these horrendous moments, in which all man's earthly possessions were vanishing and all nature was being threatened with extinction, the human spirit itself seemed to unfold like the loveliest of flowers. In the fields, as far as the eye could see, men and women of every social station could be seen lying side by side, princes and beggars, ladies and peasant women, government officials and labourers, friars and nuns – all pitying one another, helping one another, willingly sharing anything they might have saved to help them subsist, as if the general catastrophe had united all its survivors into one *single* family.

Instead of trivial tea-table topics of conversation about the ways of the world, everyone was now telling stories of heroic deeds: people, who had till now gone almost unnoticed in society, had shown a Roman greatness of character: countless examples of fearlessness, of blithe contempt of danger, of self-denial and saint-like sacrifice, of life thrown away without demur, as if it were the most insignificant of possessions and could be recovered in the twinkling of an eye. Indeed, since there was no one who on that day had not experienced something moving or had himself not performed some generous deed, the pain in every heart was mingled with so much sweet joy that Josefa felt it could not be established whether the sum of general well-being had not increased on the one hand, as much as it had dwindled on the other.

When they had both finished pondering these matters in silence, Jerónimo took Josefa's arm, and with inexpressible joy walked her up and down beneath the shady boughs of the pomegranate trees. He told her that, given the present mood and general upheaval, he no longer intended to set sail for Europe; that he would venture to appeal directly to the Viceroy who, should he be still alive, had always looked upon his cause with favour; and that he hoped (at this point he kissed her) to remain with her in Chile. Josefa replied that similar thoughts had occurred to her; that she no longer doubted she would be able to placate her father, were he still alive; but that, instead of pleading for mercy, she suggested it would be wiser to go to La Concepción and initiate by letter reconciliation proceedings with the Viceroy from there, where they would in any case be in reach of the port, from where, if their negotiations were successful, they could easily return to Santiago. Jerónimo, after brief reflection, approved the wisdom of these precautions, strolled with her a little along the paths, looked with happy anticipation towards their future, and then rejoined the company.

By now it was afternoon; the wandering refugees, since the tremors had finally abated, had grown somewhat calmer, and the news now spread that a solemn mass would be read in the Dominican church, the only one the earthquake had spared, by the prior of the monastery, who would implore Heaven to avert further disasters.

People were already setting out from all directions and pouring into the city. One of Don Fernando's party asked whether they too should not join in this solemn celebration and general procession. Doña Isabel recalled, with some emotion, the terrible calamity the church had suffered on the previous day; pointed out that such services of thanksgiving would certainly be repeated, and that one could celebrate with greater joy and tranquillity when the danger had receded. Josefa now leapt enthusiastically to her feet, declared that she had never felt a stronger urge to prostrate herself before her Maker than at this very time, when His incomprehensible and sublime power was being made so manifest. Doña Elvira agreed wholeheartedly. She insisted that they should hear the Mass and called upon Don Fernando to lead the way, whereupon everyone, including Doña Isabel, rose from their seats. But when the latter was seen making preparations for her departure with hesitation and a panting heart, and was asked what was wrong, she replied that she was full of a vague foreboding that she could not name. Doña Elvira soothed her and suggested that she remain behind with her and her sick father. 'Would you, then, be kind enough, Doña Isabel, to relieve me of this little darling who, as you can see, has attached himself to me again.' 'Of course,' replied Doña Isabel, and reached out for him; but when the baby screamed at this violation of his rights and would not agree to it on any terms, Josefa said with a smile that she would keep him, and kissed him till he was quiet again. Charmed by her great dignity and grace, Don Fernando now offered her his arm; Jerónimo, carrying little Felipe, escorted Doña Constanza; the others, who had joined the party, followed behind, and in this order the procession set off towards the town.

They had hardly walked fifty paces when Doña Isabel, who had been whispering most animatedly to Doña Elvira, called out: 'Don Fernando,' and ran forward in some turmoil to join the procession. Don Fernando stopped and turned round;

he waited for her, without letting go of Josefa's arm and asked her, when she remained standing some distance away as if expecting him to come and meet her, what she wanted. Whereupon Doña Isabel approached them, albeit with apparent reluctance, and whispered a few words in his ear in such a way that Josefa could not hear them. 'Well' asked Don Fernando, 'and what harm can come of that?' Doña Isabel, looking quite distraught, continued to whisper angrily into his ear. Don Fernando flushed with displeasure, replied: 'That will do! Tell Doña Elvira not to worry,' and continued to escort Josefa into the town.

Having arrived at the Dominican church they were greeted by splendid organ music and a huge crowd thronging inside the building. The multitude extended far beyond the portals into the square outside the church; while inside small boys had climbed up the walls and were perching alongside the paintings, with their caps clutched expectantly in their hands. All the candelabra were blazing with light, the pillars were casting mysterious shadows in the gathering dusk, the stained glass of the great rose window at the far end of the church glowed like the evening sun that illuminated it, and silence reigned throughout the congregation, now that the organ was silent, as if each soul had been struck dumb. Never had such religious fervour risen to heaven from a Christian cathedral as on that day from the Dominican church at Santiago, and no hearts glowed with warmer fervour than those of Jerónimo and Josefa!

The celebration began with a sermon delivered from the pulpit by one of the canons, clad in ceremonial robes. Raising high up to heaven his trembling hands enveloped by the wide sleeves of his surplice, he began at once to give praise and glory and thanks that in this devastated corner of the world men and women should still exist who were able to stammer their thanks to God. He described how, at a sign from the Almighty, the catastrophe had happened; the Last Judgement, he said, could not be more terrible; and when, pointing to a crack in the cathedral wall, he called yesterday's earthquake a mere harbinger of that dreadful day, a shudder ran through the whole congregation. His priestly eloquence now focused on the moral depravity of the town: he accused it of abominations that even Sodom and Gomorrah had not known; and it was only due to God's infinite forbearance that the town had not been expunged from the face of the earth.

When the canon then described in detail the outrage that had been perpetrated in the gardens of the Carmelite convent, the hearts of our two wretched friends, lacerated as they already were by the preacher's words, were pierced to the quick. He condemned as godless the indulgence with which society had treated the outrage, and in a digression filled with imprecations he even mentioned the two sinners by name and consigned their souls to all the princes of hell! 'Don Fernando!' cried Doña Constanza, plucking Jerónimo by the arm. But Fernando answered as emphatically and yet as surreptitiously as possible: 'Do not say a word, Doña, do not even move, but pretend you are about to faint, and we will leave the church.' But before Doña Constanza could even carry out this ingenious plan of escape, a voice rang out, interrupting the canon's sermon: 'Stand well away, citizens of Santiago, here they are, those two godless sinners!' And when, as a wide circle of people backed away in horror, another terrified voice asked: 'Where?', a third man replied: 'Here!' and, filled with holy indignation and barbarity, seized Josefa by the hair with such violence that she and Don Fernando's child would have fallen to the ground if he had not supported her. 'Are you mad?' cried the young man, putting his arm round Josefa, 'I am Don Fernando Ormez, the son of the commandant of this city, whom you all know.' 'Don Fernando Ormez?' exclaimed a man close by, a cobbler who had worked for Josefa and knew her as well as he knew her little feet. 'Who is the father of this child?' he asked, turning with insolent defiance to Asterón's daughter. Don Fernando turned pale at the question. He looked furtively at Jerónimo and then surveyed the congregation to see if there was anyone who might know him. Impelled by the horrific situation, Josefa cried out: 'This is not my child, Master Pedrillo;' and looking at Don Fernando in endless anguish she added: 'This young gentleman is Don Fernando Ormez, son of the commandant of this city, whom you all know!' The cobbler asked: 'Which of you citizens knows this young man?' And several of the bystanders repeated: 'Let him who knows Jerónimo Rugera step forward!' It so happened that at this very moment little Juan, frightened by the uproar, began to struggle in Josefa's arms and reach out for Don Fernando. 'He *is* the father!' cried a voice; 'He *is* Jerónimo Rugera!' yelled another; while a third voice screamed: 'These *are* the blasphemers!' And all the Christians in that temple of Jesus shouted in unison: 'Stone them! Stone them!' At which point Jerónimo cried out: 'Stop! You monsters! If you are looking for Jerónimo Rugera, he is here! Free that man, who is innocent!'

The furious mob, confused by Jerónimo's words, faltered; several hands released Don Fernando; and when at that moment a naval officer of high rank pushed his way hurriedly through the crowd and asked: 'Don Fernando Ormez! What has happened to you?', the latter, now quite free, replied with truly heroic presence of mind: 'These are nothing but murderous villains, Don Alonzo! If this worthy gentleman had not calmed this raging rabble by pretending to be Jerónimo Rugera, I should have been a dead man. Be so kind as to arrest him and this young lady, for their own protection; and arrest this scoundrel too,' he added, seizing Master Pedrillo, 'for it was he who started the whole furore!' The cobbler shouted: 'Don Alonzo Onoreja, I ask you on your conscience, is this girl not Josefa Asterón?' And when Don Alonzo, who knew Josefa very well, hesitated before replying, and several people, enraged once more, cried out: 'It is her! It is her! Kill her!', Josefa placed little Felipe, whom Jerónimo had been carrying, and little Juan in Don Fernando's arms, and said: 'Go, Don Fernando, save your two children and leave us to our fate!'

Don Fernando took both children and said that he would sooner die than allow any member of his party to come to harm. Having asked the naval officer to lend him his sword, he offered Josefa his arm, and told the couple behind to follow him. And, as the people showed sufficient respect, they did indeed make their way out of the church, and thought themselves saved. But hardly had they set foot in the forecourt, which also heaved with humanity, than a voice from the frenzied crowd that had pursued them cried out: 'Citizens! This is Jerónimo Rugera, for I am his own father!', and clubbed him with a mighty blow to the ground at Doña Constanza's side. 'Jesus Maria!' screamed Doña Constanza, as she rushed up to her brother-in-law; but another cry immediately rang out: 'Convent strumpet!' and a second blow from another quarter struck her down lifeless next to Jerónimo. 'Monsters!' came the cry from an unidentified bystander, 'this was Doña Constanza Xares!' 'Why did they lie to us?' retorted the cobbler. 'Find the right one, and kill her!' Don Fernando, seeing Constanza's corpse beside him, seethed with rage; he drew and brandished his sword and slashed at the fanatical murderer who had fanned these atrocities and who, had he not stepped aside, would have been cut in two by the furious blow. But since he could not quell the surging throng that pressed in on him, Josefa cried out: 'Farewell, Don Fernando, farewell children! Murder me, you bloodthirsty tigers!' and threw herself amongst them to put an end to the fighting. Master Pedrillo clubbed her to the ground. Then, spattered from head to foot with her blood, he shrieked: 'Send her bastard to join her in hell!' and pressed forward once more, his appetite for carnage not yet sated.

Don Fernando, this godlike hero, was now leaning against the church wall; on his left arm he held the children, in his right hand his sword. With each blow he scythed one of his assailants down; a lion could not have put up a better defence. Seven of the butcherers lay dead at his feet, and the ringleader of the satanic rabble himself was wounded. But Master Pedrillo would not relent until he had seized one of the infants by the legs, whirled it in the air above his head and dashed it against a pillar of the church. Silence now fell and the whole crowd withdrew. Don Fernando, seeing little Juan at his feet with his brains pouring from his skull, raised his eyes to heaven with indescribable anguish.

The naval officer now rejoined him, tried to comfort him and assured him that, though he himself for various reasons had failed to intervene in this terrible incident, he now bitterly regretted it; but Don Fernando said that there was no cause for reproach, and merely asked for his help in removing the bodies. They were all now carried, under cover of falling darkness, to Don Alonzo's house; and Don Fernando followed, his bitter tears falling onto little Felipe's face, as he cradled him in his arms. He also spent the night with Don Alonzo and, by little prevarications, managed for some time to keep the full extent of the calamity from his wife; firstly, because she was ill, and also because he was not sure how she would judge his own conduct in the episode. But it was not long before this excellent lady was weeping out her maternal grief, having accidentally learned from a visitor exactly what had happened; and one morning, with still-wet eyes, she threw her arms round her husband's neck and kissed him. Don Fernando and Doña Elvira then adopted the little stranger as their own son; and when Don Fernando compared Felipe with Juan, and the ways in which he had acquired them both, it almost seemed to him that he had cause to be glad.

The Foundling

Antonio Piachi, a wealthy Roman property dealer, was required from time to time to undertake lengthy journeys on business. Usually he would leave behind his young wife, Elvira, in the care of her relatives. One of these journeys took him and his eleven-year-old son, Paolo, the child of his first marriage, to Ragusa. It so happened that a plague-like disease had just broken out and was spreading great panic throughout the city and the surrounding area. Piachi, who only discovered the news when he had already set out, stopped on the outskirts of the town to enquire about it. But when he heard that the epidemic was growing more serious each day and that they were thinking of closing the gates, concern for his son prevailed over all other business plans: he hired horses and departed.

On reaching the open countryside, he noticed beside his carriage a boy who was holding out one of his hands, pleadingly, in the manner of a beggar, and who seemed to be in great distress. Piachi told the coachman to stop, and the boy, when asked what he wanted, replied innocently that he was contagious, that the authorities were pursuing him to take him to the hospital where his father and mother had already died; and, calling on all the saints, he begged Piachi to take him with him and not leave him behind to perish in the town. As he spoke he grabbed the old man's hand, pressed it and kissed it and covered it with tears. Piachi's first reaction was one of horror, and he was about to hurl the boy as far away from him as possible, when the latter turned pale and fell unconscious to the ground. The kind old man's pity was stirred: he and his son got out of the carriage, lifted the boy on board and drove off, although he had not the slightest idea of what to do with him.

He was still negotiating with the innkeeper at the first coach station how he could best get rid of him when the police, who had got wind of the affair, gave orders for him to be arrested; and he, his son and the sick boy, whose name was Nicolo, were now transported under guard back to Ragusa. No matter how much Piachi railed against the cruelty of such a decision, it was all to no avail. When they arrived in Ragusa, all three of them were handed over to a bailiff and taken to the hospital where Piachi remained healthy and the boy Nicolo recovered from the disease; Piachi's son, however, the eleven-year-old Paolo, became infected and died within three days.

The city gates were now opened once more and Piachi, having buried his son, obtained permission from the police to leave. Shaken with grief, he was just climbing into his carriage when, seeing the empty seat beside him, he took out his handkerchief to let his tears flow; it was then that Nicolo, cap in hand, approached the carriage and wished him a good journey. Piachi leant out and asked him, in a voice broken by convulsive sobbing, whether he would like to travel with him. The boy, as soon as he had understood the old man, nodded and said: 'Oh, very much indeed!' And since the hospital authorities, on being asked by the property dealer whether the boy might be permitted to join him, smiled and assured him that the boy was an orphan and would be missed by no one, Piachi, greatly moved, lifted him into the carriage and took him back to Rome in place of his son.

It was not until they were on the road outside the gates that Piachi took a good look at the boy. He was handsome in a most individual and statuesque way, his black locks hung down from his forehead in simple strands, darkening a serious and clever face that never changed its expression. The old man asked him several questions to which the boy gave short answers; uncommunicative and introverted, he sat in the corner of the carriage with his hands in his pockets, looking pensively at each object which flashed past outside the window. From time to time, quietly and noiselessly, he would take handfuls of nuts out of his pockets and, while Piachi wiped the tears from his eyes, crack them open with his teeth.

Having arrived in Rome and given a brief explanation of what had happened, Piachi introduced the boy to his excellent young wife Elvira, who wept bitter tears at the thought of her young stepson Paolo, whom she had loved dearly; nonetheless, she embraced Nicolo, though he stood stiff and aloof before her, showed him the bed in which Paolo had slept and gave him all his clothes to wear. Piachi sent him to school where he studied reading, writing and arithmetic, and since he, quite understandably, had become all the fonder of the boy through having acquired him at such a price, he adopted him as a son after only a few weeks and with the agreement of the kind-hearted Elvira, who could now entertain no hope of bearing the old man any more children. Later, having dismissed a clerk with whom he was for various reasons dissatisfied, he was delighted to see that Nicolo, whom he had appointed in the clerk's place, managed all his complicated business affairs in a most active and beneficial manner. Piachi, who was a sworn enemy of all bigotry, could find no fault with him except for the way he associated with the monks of the Carmelite monastery, who showered him with affection on account of the considerable fortune which he would one day inherit from the old man; and Elvira's only reservation was that Nicolo seemed to display a precocious predilection for the fair sex. At the age of fifteen he had already, during his visits to these monks, been seduced by the wiles of a certain Xaviera Tartini, the bishop's concubine; and even though, on Piachi's stern insistence, he had ended this liaison, Elvira had reason to believe that Nicolo was far from being a model of abstinence in these precarious matters. When, however, at the age of twenty, Nicolo married Elvira's niece, Constanza Parquet, a charming young Genoese lady who had been educated in Rome under her aunt's supervision, this particular affliction seemed to have been cut off at source; both parents declared themselves satisfied with him, and to give proof of this, they provided for him in a most sumptuous way, putting at his disposal a considerable part of their beautiful and spacious house. In short, when Piachi had reached the age of sixty, he took the final and most generous step that a benefactor could take: he bequeathed to him, in a court of law, the entire fortune on which his property business was based, retaining only a small capital for himself, and, with the splendid and faithful Elvira, who had few wishes in the world, withdrew into retirement.

There was a silent and melancholy side to Elvira's nature, resulting from a touching episode that had occurred in her childhood. Her father, Filippo Parquet, an affluent Genoese dyer, lived in a house on a massive stone embankment that looked out onto the sea, as was necessary for his trade; huge beams, built into the gable, on which the dyed cloths were hung, projected for several metres over the sea. On one ill-fated night fire broke out in the house and the flames spread at once to all the rooms, as though the building were made of pitch and sulphur. The thirteen-year-old Elvira, terrified by the blaze that engulfed her, fled from staircase to staircase and found herself, without knowing how, standing on one of these beams. The poor child, suspended between heaven and earth, had no idea how to save herself: behind her the blazing gable, fanned by the wind, was already eating away at the beam; beneath her raged the immense, desolate, terrible sea. She was just about to commend herself to all the saints, choose the lesser of two evils and leap into the water, when suddenly a young Genoese of patrician stock appeared in the doorway, threw his cloak over the beam, took her in his arms and with as much courage as skill lowered himself, and her, into the sea, by clinging to one of the damp cloths that dangled from the beam. They were both rescued by gondolas in the harbour and carried ashore to the jubilation of the people. But it turned out that a stone falling from the cornice had struck and severely wounded the young hero on the head as he made his way through the house, and it was not long before he lost consciousness and collapsed. He was transported to the villa of his father, the Marquis, who, when it became clear that his son was taking a long time to recover, summoned doctors from all over Italy who repeatedly trepanned his son's skull and removed several pieces of bone; but by a mysterious stroke of fate all their skill was in vain. Elvira, who had come to nurse him at his mother's request, held his hand, but he only rarely showed any signs of life; and after three years of great pain, during which the girl did not leave his side, he clasped her hand for one last time and passed away.

Piachi, who had business connections with this gentleman's family and met Elvira in the Marquis' house while she was nursing his son, married her two years later, and took great care never to mention the young man's name or recall him to her in any way, because he knew that it would shatter her delicate and sensitive nature. The slightest circumstance that reminded her, even remotely, of the period when this young man had suffered and died for her sake, always moved her to tears – after which it was impossible to comfort or quiet her; she would simply go off on her own and no one would follow her, for experience told them that the only effective remedy was to let her cry out her grief in solitude. Only Piachi knew the cause of these strange and frequent fits, for never in her life had she uttered a single word about the episode. It had become the custom to attribute these fits to a nervous disorder, the aftermath of a high fever she had succumbed to soon after her marriage – and such an explanation put an end to any further enquiries.

Nicolo, despite his father's prohibition, had never completely severed his connection with Xaviera Tartini, and had on one occasion, without his wife's knowledge and under the pretence of visiting a friend, arranged a secret rendezvous with her at the carnival. Late at night, when everyone was asleep, he returned home wearing the costume of a Genoese cavalier – a disguise that he had chosen by chance. It so happened the old man had been feeling unwell that night, and that Elvira, in the absence of servants, having got out of bed to help him, had entered the dining-room to fetch him a bottle of vinegar. She had just opened the corner cupboard and was standing on a chair to search among the glasses and carafes, when Nicolo gently pushed open the door and, sporting a plumed hat, a cloak and sword, and carrying a candle he had lit in the hall, walked through the dining-room. Innocently, without noticing Elvira, he had just reached his bedroom door when, to his bewilderment, he saw that it was locked; Elvira, standing behind him on the chair, with bottles and glasses in her hand, caught sight of him and, as if struck by invisible lightning, immediately fell onto the panelled floor. Nicolo, pale with horror, turned round and was on the point of rushing to the poor woman's assistance, but since the noise she had made would certainly bring Piachi to the scene, and since he was anxious to avoid the old man's reproaches, he snatched, with a mixture of panic and haste, the bunch of keys that hung from her waist, found one which opened the door, threw the remaining keys back into the dining-room and vanished. Ill as he was, Piachi had soon jumped out of bed, lifted her up and rung for the servants who appeared with lights; and it was not long before Nicolo, too, appeared in his dressing-gown and asked what had happened. But Elvira, her tongue paralysed with terror, was unable to utter a word, and as there was no other person who could have answered his question, the incident remained wreathed in mystery. Trembling in every limb, Elvira was carried to bed, where for several days she lay ill with a high fever; her natural good health, however, enabled her to recover from this chance incident tolerably well, although it left her strangely depressed.

A year had passed when Constanza, Nicolo's wife, died in childbirth, together with the infant she had borne. This loss was doubly regrettable: not only had this virtuous and well-educated woman perished, but her death had given Nicolo fresh opportunity to indulge his two vices – his bigotry and his predilection for the opposite sex. Under the pretext of seeking consolation, he began once more to frequent for days on end the cells of the Carmelite monks, although it was known that he had shown his wife little love or fidelity while she had lived. Indeed, Constanza had not yet been buried when Elvira, entering Nicolo's room one evening to make arrangements for the funeral, had surprised him with a girl whom, by her painted face and petticoats, she recognised only too well as Xaviera Tartini's chambermaid. Elvira lowered her gaze, turned and left the room without a word. She said nothing to Piachi or anyone else about the incident, and contented herself with weeping and kneeling with a heavy heart by the body of Constanza, who had loved Nicolo passionately. But it so happened that Piachi, who had been out in the town, encountered the girl as he entered his house; and knowing full well what her business here had been, he confronted her sternly and managed, half by subterfuge and half by force, to get hold of the letter that she was carrying. He went to his room to read it and found that it was, as he had suspected, an urgent message from Nicolo to Xaviera, requesting her to appoint a time and place for the rendezvous that he so longed for. Piachi sat down and, disguising his handwriting, replied in Xaviera's name: 'At once, before dark, in the Church of Santa Maria Maddalena'. He sealed the note with an unfamiliar crest and had it delivered to Nicolo's room, as if he had just received it from the lady. The trick worked; Nicolo immediately took his cloak and, forgetting about Constanza who had been laid out in her coffin, left the house. Piachi, greatly offended, now cancelled the solemn funeral which had been arranged for the following day, gave orders to a few bearers to shoulder the laid-out corpse just as it was and, accompanied only by Elvira, himself and a few relatives, to bury it with the utmost secrecy in the vault of Santa Maria Maddalena. Nicolo, wrapped in his cloak, waited in the narthex of the church and, astonished to see the approach of a funeral procession made up of familiar faces, asked Piachi, who was following the coffin, what this meant and who it was they were burying. But Piachi, with prayer-book in hand and without looking up, merely answered: 'Xaviera Tartini', at which point the corpse was uncovered once more, as though Nicolo had not been present, blessed by all the mourners, lowered into the tomb and closed.

This deeply humiliating episode ignited in Nicolo's heart a raging hatred for Elvira; for he believed her to be responsible for the disgrace her husband had inflicted on him in the full gaze of the public. Piachi did not speak to him for several days; but since Nicolo needed his stepfather's favour and goodwill in connection with Constanza's estate, he felt obliged one evening to seize the old man's hand with every appearance of repentance, and vow to renounce Xaviera once and for all and without delay. But he was little minded to keep this promise; indeed, he merely became more and more defiant in the face of opposition, and cunningly evaded the good old man's vigilance. Elvira, meanwhile, had never seemed to him more beautiful than when, to his devastation, she had opened his door and closed it again at the sight of the maid. The indignation, which had caused her cheeks to blush, bestowed infinite charm on her gentle face that only rarely showed any emotion; it seemed incredible to him that she, with so many enticements, should not occasionally tread that same path of indulgence, for which she had just punished him so shamefully. He glowed with desire, if ever this came about, to treat her in the same way that she had treated him and inform her husband; and all he now needed was the opportunity to carry out such a plan.

On one occasion – Piachi had just left the house – he was passing Elvira's door when, to his bewilderment, he heard voices in her room. An insidious hope suddenly flashed through his mind; he stooped to eavesdrop through the keyhole and – behold! what should he see but Elvira, in a pose of utter ecstasy, prostrated at someone's feet; although he could not recognise the person, he quite clearly heard her whisper the name 'Colino' with ardent passion. With pounding heart, he took up a position in the window alcove of the corridor from where, without betraying his intention, he could observe the entrance to the room; and it was not long before he thought, hearing the bolt being carefully drawn back, that the exquisite moment had come when he could unmask the hypocrite; but instead of the expected stranger, it was Elvira who emerged from the room, utterly alone, casting a calm and detached look at him as she moved away. She held a piece of handwoven cloth under her arm and, having locked the room with one of the keys that dangled from her waist, she walked with great composure downstairs with one hand on the banister. Nicolo considered this pretence, this hypocritical detachment to be the height of insolence and cunning, and hardly had she vanished from view when he ran to fetch a master-key with which, having looked cautiously about him, he opened the bedroom door. But he was astonished to find the room quite empty, and, though he searched every nook and cranny, he could not find a single trace of a man except a life-sized portrait of a young cavalier which hung in an alcove behind a red silk curtain, lit by a special lamp. Nicolo, without knowing why, was startled and a host of thoughts crossed his mind as he faced the portrait, which stared at him with its wide-open eyes. But before he could control and order his thoughts, he was seized with apprehension that Elvira would discover his presence and punish him; more than a little bewildered, he closed the bedroom door again and withdrew.

The more he pondered this strange incident, the more importance he attached to what he had discovered, and the more insistent and eager his curiosity became. For he had had an uninhibited view of Elvira's whole posture, as she had rested on her knees, and there was no doubt in his mind that the figure before whom she had prostrated herself was none other than the young nobleman on the canvas. Overcome with disquiet, he went to Xaviera Tartini and told her of his strange experience. Xaviera was as keen as Nicolo to discredit Elvira, since she blamed her for all the difficulties she encountered in her liaison, and she expressed the wish to see the portrait in the bedroom. She could boast of an extensive acquaintance among the Italian nobility, and if the young man in question had spent any time in Rome and was of any importance, it was more than likely that she would know him. As luck would have it, it was not long before Piachi and his wife went into the country one Sunday to visit a relative, and as soon as the coast was clear Nicolo rushed off to Xaviera, whom he now escorted, together with her small daughter by the cardinal, into Elvira's room, on the pretext that she was a lady who wished to view the paintings and embroideries. But Nicolo was utterly astonished when the child, whose name was Clara, exclaimed, as soon as he had drawn back the curtain: 'Goodness gracious, Signor Nicolo, that's a picture of you!' Xaviera said nothing. The longer she looked at the portrait, the more it bore a remarkable likeness to him – especially when she pictured him, as well she might, in the Genoese costume he had worn a few months ago, when they had met secretly at the carnival. Nicolo attempted to laugh off the sudden embarrassment that came over him and coloured his cheeks; he kissed the little girl and said: 'It's true, dear Clara, it resembles me as much as you resemble the man who thinks he is your father!' But Xaviera, stirred by bitter pangs of jealousy, shot him a look; and, stepping in front of the mirror, said that it was all the same to her who the person was; whereupon she took leave of him somewhat coldly, and left the room.

As soon as Xaviera had withdrawn, Nicolo fell into a state of feverish excitement over what had passed. He recalled with great delight the strange and violent turmoil into which his fanciful appearance had thrown Elvira on the night of the carnival. The thought that he might have aroused a great passion in this paragon of womanly virtue was almost as precious to him as the desire to take revenge on her; and as he now had the prospect of gratifying both desires at once, he waited impatiently for Elvira to return and for the moment when a single gaze into her eyes would dispel all his doubts and crown all his hopes. Only one thing clouded his elation, and that was the distinct recollection that the kneeling Elvira, when he had eavesdropped on her through the keyhole, had addressed the picture as 'Colino'; and yet there was something about the sound of this name, which was not exactly common in Italy, that filled his heart with the sweetest of dreams; and when faced with the choice of believing either his eyes or his ears, he naturally inclined to the evidence that flattered most his desire.

Several days later Elvira returned from the country, where she had been staying with a cousin; and since she was busy attending to a young kinswoman she had brought back with her who wanted to see Rome, she cast only a fleeting and insignificant look at Nicolo, as he very graciously helped her out of the carriage. Several weeks were now devoted to the entertainment of her guest, during which the house was in an unwonted state of excitement; they visited places in and outside the city which might have been of interest to a young and lively girl; and Nicolo who, because he was busy in the office, was not invited to take part in any of these outings, began once more to harbour the keenest resentment against Elvira. His thoughts turned again to the unknown man whom she idolised in clandestine devotion, and bitterness tormented his soul; and when at last his long-held wish was fulfilled and the young kinswoman finally departed one evening, his depraved heart suffered even greater torment when Elvira, instead of speaking to him, sat in silence for an hour at the dining-room table and busied herself with some domestic work. It so happened that Piachi, a few days earlier, had been searching for a box of little ivory letters with which Nicolo had learnt to read as a boy and which the old man, since no one needed them now, wished to give to a small child in the neighbourhood. The maidservant, who had been told to look for them among many other discarded objects, had only managed to find the six letters that formed Nicolo's name, presumably because the others, having less relevance to the boy, were of less interest and had some time ago been thrown out. Nicolo picked up these letters, which had been lying for several days on the table at which he now sat brooding, and had begun to play with them when he discovered – by chance, because he had never in his life been so astonished – that they spelt the name 'Colino'. Nicolo, who had been unaware that such an anagram of his name existed, was once again seized by the wildest hopes and cast an uncertain and anxious gaze at Elvira, as she sat beside him. The correspondence between the two words seemed to him more than mere coincidence; suppressing his delight, he pondered the significance of his strange discovery, slipped his hands from the table and waited with pounding heart for the moment when Elvira would look up and see the name there, as clear as daylight. He was not to be disappointed; for no sooner had she, in an idle moment, noticed the new arrangement of the letters and unwittingly leant forward – she was a little short-sighted – to read them, than she glanced at Nicolo, as he looked down at them with feigned insouciance, with a look of strange apprehension; she took up her work again with a look of indescribable sadness and, thinking herself unobserved, wept copious tears that fell one after another onto her lap, as her face flushed a gentle red. Nicolo, who, without looking at her, was observing all these signs of emotion, was no longer in any doubt that she had merely been concealing his own name by this spelling. He observed her stretch out her hand and gently scramble the letters, and his wild hopes seemed to be confirmed, as she stood up, laid her sewing to one side and disappeared into her bedroom. He was on the point of leaving his seat to follow her when Piachi entered and, having enquired as to where she might be, was told by one of the maidservants that she was not feeling well and had gone to lie down. Piachi, without appearing unduly alarmed, turned and went to her room to see how she was faring; when he returned fifteen minutes later, he announced that she would not appear for dinner, and did not mention the matter again. Nicolo, recalling the many mysterious scenes of this kind that he had witnessed, felt now that he held the key to their meaning.

The next morning, as he wallowed in his shameful joy and considered how he might best exploit his new discovery, he received a note from Xaviera in which she asked him to come and see her, since she had some interesting information to reveal about Elvira. Xaviera, as the bishop's protégée, was on most intimate terms with the monks of the Carmelite monastery; and since it was to this monastery that his foster-mother went to confession, he had no doubt that Xaviera had managed to glean some information about the secret history of her feelings which would benefit his unnatural desires. But an unpleasant surprise was in store for him, because Xaviera, having greeted him with a strangely mischievous look, drew him down with a smile onto the divan where she sat, and declared quite simply that the object of Elvira's love was a man who had for the past twelve years been slumbering in his grave. The original of the portrait he had discovered in her bedroom in the alcove behind the red silk curtain was Aloysius, Marquis of Montferrat, who had been educated in Paris at the house of his uncle, to whom he was known as Collin, a nickname that had later in Italy been playfully changed to Colino – and he was the young Genoese nobleman who had died from his wounds after he had so valiantly rescued her from the fire when she was a child. Xaviera added that it was her duty to ask Nicolo to refrain from making any use of this secret, since it had been entrusted to her in the Carmelite monastery, under a vow of absolute discretion, by a person who himself had no right to it. Nicolo, alternately flushing red and turning pale, assured her that she had nothing to fear; and being quite incapable of concealing from her mischievous looks the commotion which this disclosure had caused him, he picked up his hat on the pretext of having business to attend to and, with an unpleasant twitch of his upper lip, took his leave.

Shame, lust and revenge now conjoined in his mind to hatch the most despicable deed ever committed. He was aware that Elvira's pure soul could only be conquered through deception; and as soon as Piachi, who had gone to the country for a few days, left the coast clear, he took steps to execute the satanic plan that he had devised. He procured once more the identical costume in which he had appeared to Elvira a few months earlier, when late at night he had secretly returned from the carnival; and having put on the cloak, doublet and feathered hat of Genoese cut, exactly as the figure in the portrait wore them, he stealthily slipped into Elvira's room shortly before she retired, hung a black cloth over the picture in the alcove and awaited, staff in hand, in the very same posture of the young nobleman on the canvas, the object of Elvira's adoration. And with the insight provided by his shameful passion, he had surmised correctly: for it was not long before she entered, and no sooner had she quietly and calmly undressed and drawn back, as she always did, the silk curtain of the alcove to behold him, than with a cry of 'Colino!

My beloved!' she fell senseless onto the wooden floor. Nicolo stepped from the alcove; he stood for a moment drinking in her beauty and gazing at her delicate figure that now grew pale beneath the kiss of death; but as there was no time to lose, he soon gathered her up into his arms, ripped the black cloth from the portrait and carried her to the bed in the corner of the room. He then went to bolt the door, but found it already locked; and confident that, even after recovering her confused senses, she would submit to his fantastical and seemingly supernatural appearance, he now returned to the bed and tried to revive her by kissing her passionately on her lips and breasts. But Fate, which always strikes in the wake of crime, had decreed that Piachi, whom the wretched Nicolo thought would be absent for another few days, should at that very moment unexpectedly return home; imagining Elvira to be asleep, he crept softly along the corridor and, as he always carried the keys with him, managed to step suddenly and noiselessly into the room. Thunderstruck, Nicolo stood rooted to the ground; and since there could be no question of concealing his evil designs, he threw himself at the old man's feet and, vowing never to look upon his wife again, implored forgiveness. And the old man did indeed seem inclined to draw a veil over the affair; rendered silent by something Elvira had whispered to him as she revived in his arms and gazed with horror at the miscreant, he merely closed the curtains of her bed, took a whip from the wall, opened the door and made it clear to Nicolo that he should leave forthwith. But the latter, realising that nothing was to be gained by such a course, suddenly stood up and, in a manner worthy of Tartuffe, declared that it was Piachi's duty to leave the house, since he, Nicolo, now possessed the necessary documents that made him the legal owner, and that he would assert his rights against all comers! Piachi could not believe his ears; as though disarmed by such outrageous impudence, he put down the whip, picked up his hat and stick, ran at once to the house of his old friend, the lawyer Dr Valerio, rang the bell till a maid opened the door and, having reached his friend's room, collapsed unconscious beside his bed before he could utter a word. Dr Valerio invited him, and later Elvira as well, to stay at his house, and next morning set off in haste to secure the arrest of the diabolical Nicolo whose legal position, however, was strong; and while Piachi sought vainly to dispossess Nicolo of the property which he had already made over to him, the scoundrel, furnished with his deed of settlement, flew like the wind to his friends, the Carmelite monks, and called upon them to protect him against the old fool who was now trying to evict him. In short – since he agreed to marry Xaviera, whom the Bishop wished to get rid of, evil prevailed, and the government was persuaded by this man of the church to issue a decree which confirmed Nicolo's right to the property and required Piachi to bother him no more.

It was only on the previous day that Piachi had buried the wretched Elvira who, as a result of the recent episode, had died of a high fever. Incensed by this double blow, he entered the house with the injunction in his pocket and, strengthened through rage, hurled the less robust Nicolo to the ground and smashed his brains against the wall. The servants only became aware of Piachi's presence when the deed was already done, and by the time they found him he was holding Nicolo between his knees and stuffing the injunction down his throat. Whereupon he stood up, surrendered all his weapons, was thrown into prison, tried and condemned to death by hanging.

No criminal, according to a law in the Papal States, may be led to his death before he has received absolution. Piachi, as soon as he had been condemned to die, stubbornly refused to receive absolution. After they had tried in vain to convince him, using every argument that religion had to offer, that his crime merited the death penalty, he was marched to the gallows in the hope that the sight of imminent death might scare him into remorse. One priest, with a voice like the last trump, described to him all the terrors of hell into which his soul was about to be plunged; another, holding in his hand the Body of Christ, that sacred means of redemption, was commending to him the dwellings of eternal peace. 'Will you receive the blessed gift of salvation?' they both asked him. 'Will you receive communion?' 'No,' replied Piachi. 'Why not?' 'I do not wish to be saved. I wish to descend into the deepest depths of hell. I wish to find Nicolo, who will not be in heaven, and proceed with my revenge, which could only be partially completed here on earth!' And so saying he climbed the scaffold and called upon the hangman to do his duty. The execution, however, had to be postponed and the wretched man, whom the law protected, was escorted back to prison. Similar attempts were made on three successive days, each time without success. When on the third day he once more descended the ladder without being hanged, he raised his hands in a gesture of rage and cursed the inhuman law that would not allow him to go to hell. He summoned all the devils to come and fetch him, swore that his only wish was to be condemned and damned, and vowed he would throttle the first priest he could get hold of, if that enabled him to go to hell and get his hands on Nicolo again! The Pope, when he was told of this, ordered him to be executed without absolution; with no priest to accompany him, he was strung up in utter silence in the Piazza del Popolo.

Heinrich von Kleist was born in 1777 into an old aristocratic family in Frankfurt an der Oder. Kleist received a private education in Berlin and was an enthusiastic student and musician, but at the age of fifteen, following his father, Friedrich von Kleist, who had died a few years earlier, he enlisted in the Prussian army.

Kleist experienced active service during the Wars of the Coalitions against Revolutionary France, but disliked army life and, in 1790, resigned his commission and attempted to find his place in civilian society. He studied for a time at the University of Frankfurt an der Oder and took on board a conventional Enlightenment understanding of the human journey towards self-perfection and universal knowledge. His confidence was entirely overturned, however when, in 1801, he first read Kant, whose theories of knowledge and truth led Kleist to the conclusion that the rational nature of human life and the universe was a fallacy.

This new philosophy was psychologically devastating to Kleist, but in part was responsible for his impulse to begin writing. His first works, including the popular comedy *Der zerbrochene Krug* [*The Broken Pitcher*] (1807), attracted the attention of many contemporary literary figures, among them Goethe, who, though he disliked much of Kleist's philosophy, later helped him stage his tragi-comedy *Amphitryon* (1807).

In 1807, having returned to Prussia, Kleist was mistakenly arrested as a spy. During the six months of his detention in France, he produced one of his greatest works, the tragedy *Penthesilea* (1807), a psychological work of emotional and physical conflict, running totally contrary to the cerebral classical tradition. His first short story, '*Das Erdbeben in Chili*'

['The Earthquake in Chile'] appeared shortly afterwards, and on his return to Germany, Kleist co-founded a literary journal entitled *Phöbus*, in which several of his plays and short stories were published. The journal was financially unsuccessful and was abandoned after a short time.

In 1810, Kleist enjoyed something of a resurgence as co-founder of the newspaper *Berliner Abendblätter*. When the paper failed early the next year, however, Kleist was once again left with few resources. His final play *Prinz Friedrich von Homburg* [*Prince Frederick of Homburg*] was finished in the autumn of 1811 and intended to appeal to the Prussian royal family. It was unsuccessful, however, due to the unconventional emotional depiction of the hero, and remained unpublished during Kleist's lifetime. The same year, in utter despair, Kleist formed a suicide pact with Henriette Vogel, a woman suffering from terminal cancer, and at Wannsee near Berlin, he shot her and then himself.

Richard Stokes teaches languages at Westminster School, coaches singers in the interpretation of Lieder, and gives frequent lectures on song composers. He has co-authored a number of books on German, French and Spanish song, and his singing-translations of Berg's *Wozzeck*, Wagner's *Parsifal* and Berg's *Lulu* met with great acclaim. He has also translated Kafka's *Metamorphosis* for Hesperus Press.

HESPERUS PRESS – 100 PAGES

Hesperus Press, as suggested by the Latin motto, is committed to bringing near what is far – far both in space and time. Works written by the greatest authors, and unjustly neglected or simply little known in the English-speaking world, are made accessible through new translations and a completely fresh editorial approach. Through these short classic works, each around 100 pages in length, the reader will be introduced to the greatest writers from all times and all cultures.

For more information on Hesperus Press, please visit our website: **www.hesperuspress.com**

ET REMOTISSIMA PROPE

SELECTED TITLES FROM HESPERUS PRESS

Gustave Flaubert *Memoirs of a Madman*

Alexander Pope *Scriblerus*

Ugo Foscolo *Last Letters of Jacopo Ortis*

Anton Chekhov *The Story of a Nobody*

Joseph von Eichendorff *Life of a Good-for-nothing*

Mark Twain *The Diary of Adam and Eve*

Giovanni Boccaccio *Life of Dante*

Victor Hugo *The Last Day of a Condemned Man*

Joseph Conrad *Heart of Darkness*

Edgar Allan Poe *Eureka*

Emile Zola *For a Night of Love*

Daniel Defoe *The King of Pirates*

Giacomo Leopardi *Thoughts*

Nikolai Gogol *The Squabble*

Franz Kafka *Metamorphosis*

Herman Melville *The Enchanted Isles*

Leonardo da Vinci *Prophecies*

Charles Baudelaire *On Wine and Hashish*

William Makepeace Thackeray *Rebecca and Rowena*

Wilkie Collins *Who Killed Zebedee?*

Théophile Gautier *The Jinx*

Charles Dickens *The Haunted House*

Luigi Pirandello *Loveless Love*

Fyodor Dostoevsky *Poor People*

E.T.A. Hoffmann *Mademoiselle de Scudéri*

Henry James *In the Cage*

Francis Petrarch *My Secret Book*

André Gide *Theseus*

D.H. Lawrence *The Fox*

Percy Bysshe Shelley *Zastrozzi*

Marquis de Sade *Incest*

Oscar Wilde *The Portrait of Mr W.H.*

Giacomo Casanova *The Duel*

Leo Tolstoy *Hadji Murat*

Friedrich von Schiller *The Ghost-seer*

Nathaniel Hawthorne *Rappaccini's Daughter*

Pietro Aretino *The School of Whoredom*

Honoré de Balzac *Colonel Chabert*

Thomas Hardy *Fellow-Townsmen*

Arthur Conan Doyle *The Tragedy of the Korosko*

Stendhal *Memoirs of an Egotist*

Katherine Mansfield *In a German Pension*

Giovanni Verga *Life in the Country*

Ivan Turgenev *Faust*

Theodor Storm *The Lake of the Bees*

F. Scott Fitzgerald *The Rich Boy*

Dante Alighieri *New Life*

Guy de Maupassant *Butterball*

Charlotte Brontë *The Green Dwarf*

Elizabeth Gaskell *Lois the Witch*

Joris-Karl Huysmans *With the Flow*

George Eliot *Amos Barton*

Gabriele D'Annunzio *The Book of the Virgins*

Alexander Pushkin *Dubrovsky*